THE ANGEL CAMPAIGN

KAREN BURGER

BALBOA.
PRESS

A DIVISION OF HAY HOUSE

Balboa Press books may be ordered through booksellers or by contacting:

Balboa Press
A Division of Hay House
1663 Liberty Drive
Bloomington, IN 47403
www.balboapress.com
1 (877) 407-4847

Print information available on the last page.

ISBN: 978-1-5043-9434-5 (sc)
ISBN: 978-1-5043-9435-2 (e)

Balboa Press rev. date: 12/29/2017

DEDICATION

To my husband who has given me encouragement and support to finish this book and hopefully many more. Your belief in me helps to keep me typing away. I love you very much. I can't wait for the day that you carry my books for me, as we go on our new adventures.

To my friend Tesa, who has told me all along, that this is what I should be doing. I am stepping out of my comfort zone and reaching for that goal.

And to all my friends that will be reading this book, I thank you! For without your love and support too, I wouldn't have finished.

Dear Reader,

Have you ever wondered what happens to us when we die? Is that all there is? We die, are buried and what? How about our spirits? I realize that our physical bodies stay here, are laid to rest six feet under with a marker placed so our families can remember where we are. But is there a significant area, zone, home or another plain where our spirit goes? The heart of who we are. Will we ever get to speak to our loved ones again? See them one more time?

There are many people and institutions that have an opinion on this subject. Some will agree that yes, there is life after death and others will argue absolutely not! The Bible teaches us that when one passes from his or her life on earth, that your physical body is laid to rest and your spirit rises up and when the time comes, is to be judged by God. The majority of people say we never come back.

If this is correct, then how do you explain ghost sightings or people claiming to have talked to a spirit? Are those thousands of people just crazy or is it true? Are ghosts and spirits one and the same or different? Is that feeling of someone or something watching you just your imagination or is there an explanation? That slight chill you just got while you were sitting there thinking about a loved one. Or how about your young child staring off into space and talking with no one? Would you say those are just coincidences? Are there really people with the ability to talk to a family member that has passed? Or maybe tell you something is going to happen that you yourself would not have known?

Yes, I believe there are special people with real gifts that live in this world where anything is possible.

Many Happy Readings,
Karen Burger

INTRODUCTION

I n life there are many unexplainable incidents. Things that happen to ordinary people and are ignored or excused for one thing or another. There are extraordinary people in this world that have been given the gift of sight, predictions, telepathy, and psychic abilities. We call them mediums, fortune-tellers, mind readers, ghost whispers, clairvoyants or crystal gazers. Take your pick. There are some slight differences between these groups, as not all can do the same things.

A psychic/medium is a person with a special talent to see things others cannot. They can also speak through Spirit, which is their guide, to others that have passed away. They can answer questions you ask about something personal. Questions like, will your house sell? Will you find love? Is that job going to work out? Should you buy a piece of property? The questions are endless of what you can ask. The answers may not always make sense at the time, but eventually they will. Or you may understand what it means at that precise moment.

Clairvoyance is a gift that can see in the future. They have precognition. This is an ability to actually perceive or see a future event through extrasensory perception before it happens. Some clairvoyants have precognitive dreams, too. These are dreams that appear to predict the future through a sixth sense. A way of accessing future information that is unrelated to any existing knowledge acquired through normal means.

Telepathy is a gift of feeling perception, passion or affliction through purported transmission of information from one person to another without using any of our known sensory channels or physical interaction, like talking. Yes, mind to mind.

It was said, that Abraham Lincoln was purported to have had the precognitive ability. Before his assassination, he told his wife and close friends about a dream he had. In the dream he was at a funeral inside the White House. He walked over to a soldier standing guard over the casket and asked, "Who is inside the casket?" to which the soldier replied, "The President of the United States, sir." One week later President Abraham Lincoln was assassinated.

CHAPTER 1

My mornings begin like every other day. Drinking coffee, listening to the different sounds of nature waking up and giving my thanks to God for another glorious day. It amazes me when I think about how He made all that we see. And with just a few spoken words. Powerful stuff to ponder. Everything feels right. The sun is peaking in and out of the clouds, there is just a hint of breeze, my business is doing well and I have my own symphony of music all around me. Ok, maybe not everyone is in tune today. It seems Mrs. Squirrel is not very happy at the moment. Boy, I wouldn't want to be on that end of the lecture! Jake and I are going to go for our morning run here shortly. But first, I need to finish my devotions.

Once I was done, I just sat there for a while longer pondering the life I have and trying to decide if I was going to go home to Alaska for the summer or stay here. I could always use the extra money that helping my family brings in, but something tells me I need to stay here at home this year. My life here in Idaho is a good one. I have a steady job that pays the bills. And my best friend lives near me. That and Jake is here. Jake is a handsome boy. He is not too tall but built pretty stout. His hair is jet black, soft to the touch and he has pretty blue eyes. He is very devoted to me and we get along so well. Jake weighs in about 95 lbs. I found him as a puppy at the local shelter my friend runs. It was love at first sight.

I never had a pet because I travel. My day job is something I do to pay the bills like I said, but, my true calling takes me to other places. I love to travel. When I first moved to Idaho I was skeptical about letting people in on what I can do. Not everyone is ok with my ability. What ability you may ask?

Hello, my name is Charlene Ensley, and I am a psychic/medium.

CHAPTER 2

Yep, you heard me. I speak to the dead that want to speak to the living. My business is called The Angel Campaign. I help people that need or want to speak to their loved ones. My goal is to bring peace to those that are still mourning their family or just need assurance about their own lives. Many people do not trust or have faith in my abilities and that is okay. Everyone is entitled to their own beliefs. But, I trust what I see, hear and feel. I believe in myself. I am at peace with my gift that I truly believe God has blessed me with. I wasn't always okay with my unique talent. It did take time to come to terms with it all.

You better believe there are many people out there who choose to say and believe that not only my gift but others are fake. That we just take from those less fortunate. And maybe there are those certain people out there that do not have a true gift of psychic ability, but I am not one of them. I have a passion and love for God and all that He has created. My beliefs are very important to me and it no longer bothers me what others think.

The mission of The Angel Campaign is to bring light and loving energy of Spirit across the globe and into the lives of every living being. With a wide range of abilities I have helped hundreds of people receive guidance that serves their highest good. I also have empathic abilities which allows me to energetically sense feelings of others and often receive information regarding their health and wellness. I truly believe that Angels are sent to help and guide us in our times of need. I have had my psychic abilities since birth. And as I grew older they developed stronger. In my heart I believe God has blessed me with this special talent so that I may help others. And I have pledged to Him, that wherever He calls me I will go.

So this is me, this is what I do. Many seek me out and others I may just run into by chance. I go wherever they may call. My loving companion Jake sometimes travels with me if I am to be gone longer than a couple days. He is a 95lb hunk of muscle with unusual blue eyes. I find that he is a great deterrent when I need him to be. It was love at first sight. And I felt that Spirit was telling me Jake is what I need and we hit it off right away. Fate is a funny thing and has a way of bringing two souls together at just the right moment. And I am a firm believer in fate.

"Jake! Let's go boy. Time to go for that run."

"Ruff! Ruff!"

Running. An evil way to exercise. Do I love it? Not really, but it keeps me in shape and most important it helps to clear my mind. Jake really enjoys it. He is my baby and I love him, so whatever he needs. Okay, maybe he isn't a baby in size but in age he is only a year and half. This big, slobbery, lovable guy is a great listener. He is very well trained with hand and voice commands. He would never hurt a fly. Well unless you were trying to hurt me, then all bets are off! The best part about running with Jake is he protects me, as my mind tends to wander while running.

Chapter 3

"So Jake, I was thinking we need to fix up the garden. You know that area you decided needed weeding? Thanks by the way. I couldn't have got so much done without your help. But in the future, let's do the job together. What do you say?"

"Ruff!"

"Yep, that's what I think too boy. Now pick up the pace! I need to get back and shower before Alice shows up."

When I run, I tend to start reminiscing about the past. Not that I intend to do it, it's just what happens. On occasion I will have a vision. But mostly I think about when my gifts started and what I went through to now. How happy I am. Life wasn't always easy. Especially being a small child with a gift that no one understood. Not even my parents knew what to do with me. Home life was not the normal, like many others. School, when I got older was a challenge. People tend to judge and run away from things they do not understand.

The earliest that I can remember seeing someone that no other person could see was around the age of 3. But my mom tells me that even as a baby, I would just stare off into space and not acknowledge anyone. They honestly thought I was deaf for quite some time. But looking back now, I truly believe that I was given this special gift at birth. Like I said the age of 3 is as soon as I can remember seeing someone. But from all accounts I was probably seeing people since I could focus.

There was this female being that I can recall very vividly. She was always shrouded in a pink, hazy light. It seemed she knew when I needed comfort and would always come to me in my time of need, mainly when I would feel frightened. She would hum a soft tune until I fell asleep. It was always the same song. I would call out for her anytime I felt upset or had anxiety. I trusted her and she made me feel loved and secure during a time of so much misunderstanding in my young life. I quit seeing her around the age of 9. I was sad, but, by then I had a little better understanding of what was happening. To this day, I still think about her and wonder if I will ever see her again or was she just sent to help me through that time in my life. That angelic being was my safe place as a small child. And I really missed her growing up.

Once I could talk, I would often see people and we would have conversations. This was a bit of a surprise for my parents. My mom was a little freaked out when she realized exactly what was happening. I have some stories that would make your hair stand up!

Children are so innocent. Their minds have yet to be trained. They are so open and honest with the spirit world around them. Kids don't judge. They talk and play with what many parents think are their imaginary friends! But in actuality, may be a spirit of a family member. Many youngsters have this gift but quit seeing spirits around the age of 9.

CHAPTER 4

Life wasn't easy for me growing up. I had my share of heartaches and disappointments from those around me that were supposed to be my friends. But as I got older, I learned to hold my tongue. I found out rather quickly that telling a person about something going on in their lives or that they were lying or revealing something that was supposed to be a secret, was not a way to win friends.

Young children and adolescent teens can be cruel with words and actions. Especially when they do not understand something. Kids are not born with hate, meanness or fear. This is taught and learned as they grow older. Maybe not directly or on purpose, but young children watch and see more than we would like. The world we live in today has many ways of showing hate and fear through all kinds of propaganda.

When I started high school, I had decided it was time to accept and fine tune my gift. Yes, I bumbled during my elementary and junior high years, making mistakes and losing friends. Many of the kids in high school were interested in what I could do, others not so much. I did not grow up with these kids so none of them knew me. There were plenty that was interested in what I could do and they called me the ghost whisperer. But then there were those that would make fun of me and do all that was possible to embarrass and continually harass me. Today, people call those kids bullies. Needless to say I ate lunch all by myself every day of my freshman year. I did not win any popularity contests, that's for sure. My cousin, whom I consider more of a sister, was always there for me when we were in elementary school and junior high, she understood everything I was going through and would always stand up for me. Boy did I miss her during high school.

It was clear that I didn't belong. Every night I would go home after school and yell at God and ask Him "Why?" I would then cry myself to sleep in the privacy of my bedroom. I had no true friends at all. Upon waking, I would have a sense of acceptance that I am different. Today would be a better day. So off to school I would go and the process would start all over again. It took me awhile to understand that I was not being punished. But that what I had was something special. Given and trusted unto me for a higher purpose.

As a young woman I didn't understand at first that what I had was supposed to be used to help others. But once I accepted my gift with my whole heart and told God that okay, here I am. It was then that I felt this great peace settle over me. And that summer, I realized what God wanted for me to do with this wonderful and rare gift I was blessed with. When school started again in the fall of my sophomore year, I met someone that ever since, has been my best friend.

When I first saw her, she was a very lonely, sad girl with no friends that I could see. Her skin was the most beautiful mocha color. She had jade green eyes and hair that seemed to go on forever. Being new to a school is hard on a teenager. I knew all about being the new kid. So I introduced myself and asked if she would like to sit with me at lunch. That was the day we became friends. I am sure she heard all the whispers from those that were out to slander me, but if she did, she chose to ignore them. I knew then, we were going to be the best of friends.

CHAPTER 5

Alice. She has been my friend now going on 20 years. When we first met, my own life was a bit chaotic. But I had given it and my gift to God and had promised to help others if I could. And my new friend had a spirit following her everywhere we went. I did not yet know who he was, just that he was attached to Alice. Our friendship was going so well. I was a little afraid to say anything to her about this. All the others always made fun of me or went off freaked out. So you can see my dilemma. Then I remembered my promise to God, so I decided that helping this spirit and hopefully Alice was what I had to do. It was a day that I wouldn't ever forget. We were walking home from school when I took the plunge. My heart couldn't take her sadness or his anymore. Even if it meant that we wouldn't be friends, I needed to try and help them both.

"Hurry up boy! Alice will be here probably sooner than later. You know how punctual she is. Some people are just that way. You and I not so much. I bet she is bringing Lucy too. You guys can play around outside while us girls have a visit."

"Ruff, ruff"

"Race you the last stretch. Go!"

When we arrived, me sucking wind and Jake running circles, Alice came around the corner of the house with Lucy.

"Why are you so out of breath," she asked.

"I raced Jake the last stretch. He won."

"Hahaha," laughed Alice. "What in the world made you think you could win him in a race?"

"Well, I was just trying to encourage him to hurry. I knew you would be early and I wanted to get here before you and take a shower. You are always so freaking punctual."

"Go. Take a shower and I will put on the tea. These two mongrels can run and play outside. I will have a snack and drink ready on the back porch when you are done. And being punctual isn't a bad thing. You should try it sometime," she laughed.

"Oh bless you," I said as I stuck my tongue out at her while walking into the bathroom.

As I hurried up and showered, I could hear Alice in the kitchen singing at the top of her lungs to something bluesy. That girl was so talented. She really missed her calling. Being a cop is something she is very good at. But if she wanted to change careers, she would be a star. It's always fun to go sing along at karaoke. I love just listening to her. She can make anyone feel good. Singing with Alice is an experience. She always encourages you and never does she make fun, even if you can't sing a lick. When I was done, I walked into the kitchen and just watched her for a few minutes. I am so blessed to have her for a friend. "So, what is on your agenda today? Are you off till Monday?" I asked, as I stirred a little raw sugar into my tea and grabbed a carrot.

"So far that is the plan. But you know how things can change. Especially being the weekend. It seems that crime rises more than during the week. Not that we have loads of it but the city is growing. How about you? Plan on staying in or do you have clients all weekend?"

"I do have some clients over the weekend but not many. Now next week I am pretty swamped! I have several new clients but many returning ones too. In two weeks I have a meeting in Montana. So I will just drive there instead of fly."

"Are you taking Jake? I really worry about you traveling alone to all those other towns. You just never know what you will run into."

"Yes, I am taking Jake with me. He does so well just sitting next to my chair. And I do make sure that whomever is setting up the meeting, knows that I bring Jake with me. I promise I will be safe."

"I just worry about you. Not everyone likes what you can do. We both know that from past experience. How was your run? I really don't understand how you like it."

"Well, I don't really like it. But it's good for Jake and truly it is good for my health too. It helps to clear my mind for the day and I feel like I have accomplished something healthy so that I can enjoy these yummy lunches you put together."

"Have you received any more letters? We are still trying to trace them but no luck yet. We didn't get any prints off them so my guess is they used gloves and a wet sponge to seal it."

"No, I haven't received anymore. I don't want to talk about them. They are too disturbing, and I don't want to ruin my good mood. It's too bad I can't read objects. We could have ended this long ago. But alas, all I can do is talk to the spirits."

"Liar! You sometimes get visions and you can read people too. I still remember when you read that one boy in school. Boy was he pissed off at you!"

"That's because I ruined his plans for prom night. There was no way I was going to let him get away with what he and his friends planned. Those girls didn't deserve that, even if they were not our favorite people. Do you ever think back to our first meeting? And look to how far we have come?"

"Yes, I do. I still remember my first reading. But most of all I remember the peace of mind you brought to me. And because of you, my family got closure, too. We found the drunk driver because you saw the license plate of the truck. My parents still have a hard time with what you do, but I know they are grateful that my brother's killer had been found."

CHAPTER 6

"I remember that day too, because I found a life friend. Someone that believed in me and didn't run from what I could do. I can still remember seeing you walk in the class room. You seemed so sad and your aura was so dark. I could sense your depression. But most of all I could see a spirit following you everywhere. I sure was afraid to say anything for some time. But, I did make a promise to God. And I knew that I had to speak to you. I am very glad that I did, because that day changed me and I know it changed you."

"Stop already. I hate to cry. You know that it's bad for my image."

"Oh you big bad cop you. It's good for the soul. You are such a bad ass anyway no one is going to mess with you. Only I know you are a big softy."

"Whatever! I am not a softy. Well, only around Jake and Lucy. They just bring out the mother instinct in me. Do you think that they will make beautiful babies?"

"Oh yes. Jake is very smart as is Lucy, and they are two built dogs. The puppies will grow into great dogs and make someone a great partner. I am glad you suggested it. You know that Jake is to me like a black cat is to a witch, right?

He can sense things, like spirits. I don't know if the puppies will be anything like that, but I do suggest that when they are ready to be partnered and trained that you let them choose. That way they will be the perfect match."

"I planned on that. I thought maybe we can keep them all out here once they are weaned. They will have much more room and the guys can come out as much as their schedules allow and get all the pups used to them. All the training stuff is out back anyway. And if you can help that would be great. I know that the police dog trainer is ecstatic already. German shepherds are usually the breed we use, but these mongrels are going to be fantastic. I take Lucy with me everywhere. It will be a bummer when she conceives and she won't be able to go. But I am happy that we have decided to do this."

"I am perfectly okay with that. Even if I am gone on a trip you are more than welcome to use the facilities."

As Alice got up to go fill the water pot, I got a vision. It was of her in a hospital gown. That's all I could see and that worried me. She is always at risk, just like all the peace officers, but this was my best friend. When I focused back on the present, she was there in front of me.

"What is wrong?"

"Nothing. Just a vision. Not a thing to worry about. But Alice? Please be careful."

She just stared at me for a moment. Trying to gauge, I am sure, how bad the vision was.

"I promise I will be careful. You know I don't ever take any unnecessary risks. Don't tell me anything either. I don't want to know when I am going to die. That is just not right.

We are not supposed to know when God has chosen for us to come home."

"Yes, I know you don't want to know. But I can and will let you know to be extra careful. Not all visions tell me when or where, you know that. So please, please be extra cautious."

"You know I will. I love my life too much to be gone just yet. But you and I both know, that my job takes me places that are not always cozy and safe. I need to be getting along. I have home chores to do and my weekly call to mom and dad will be in a few hours. Thank you for spending this time with me. I really love it when we get together and just chill. Maybe tomorrow night us girls will come out and have a wine night?"

"That sounds like a wonderful plan. I will make the dinner you choose the wine. We will decide on a movie. Love you much my friend."

"Love you much, too my friend. Now get to work you slacker."

Laughing, I watched Lucy and Alice drive away. Jake was rubbing up against me. He knew that I was feeling something and wanted to let me know that he was there. I didn't know exactly what I saw, but I knew she was in the hospital. Just not for what or when. Sometimes that can be the biggest frustration for me when I have a vision. Especially if it is about someone I care about.

"Okay Jake. It is time to get ready for my client. Be a good boy and stay out of the garden until we can do that together. Deal?"

"Ruff! Ruff!"

"Good boy. I will be in the office."

CHAPTER 7

Preparing hot water for tea is something I enjoy why waiting for the next appointment to arrive. Even if all we do is smell the fragrance of the tea, I find the clients enjoy just holding a cup of warmth in their hands. It helps them to relax and focus. I love to have tea throughout the day. But I am a coffee girl in the morning and a nice glass of chilled wine in the evenings. Once things are done and all put on the serving tray, I like to meditate before a session. This helps to clear my mind for better focus. Sometimes I will receive a visitor of the spiritual kind. Many times it will be a loved one of the new client. They know they are coming and want me to usually pass something on to them.

At the moment I am getting several spirits all vying for attention. So it is up to me to decide which to ignore and which to have a conversation with. Whomever is coming is really loved. This will be a very interesting session indeed. I heard the bell over my door chime, so I knew that my new client had arrived. I walked in to the entry hall to greet her.

"Hello. My name is Charlene. And you must be Olivia. Please, come on in. Let me take your coat for you. Go on back to the room on the left, I will go hang this up. Help yourself to the tea. I make my own blends or if you prefer there is coffee or water."

"Hello. Yes, I am Olivia. I hope you don't mind but I wanted to bring my friend so that she could listen in."

"Of course that is fine. Please help yourselves and I will return shortly."

Boy I was right. There is at least 4 different spirits trying to get my attention. But they will be ignored until I find out just what it is that Olivia wants.

"Well Olivia. What can I do for you today? I must let you know before we get started, that while I was meditating I had several spirits make themselves known. They must have sensed you were going to be speaking to me today. So I will make them all wait until you tell me just what you would like to know."

"Wow. I am speechless. This is my first time ever speaking to a medium. To be honest I am not sure if I believe any of it yet. So I am not too sure, really what I want. I know that I have a few questions and I would love to speak to my brother, but I do not want to tell you his name just yet, if that is okay with you?"

"Of course. Alright just give me a second. Hmmm. Well I can tell you I am getting pictures of desert and snow. Completely opposite sides of the world to be honest. He is showing me ice-racing and then he flashes back to a desert and tanks."

"Yes. He served in the military during Desert Storm. He was in the tank division. He loved ice-racing."

"Well, he….I am getting a strong smell of Mexican food? Yes a very strong smell of Mexican spices. He is saying he loves this kind of food."

Olivia just laughed and replied, "He loved Mexican food. And he loved cooking. He would come up with some weird dishes, but they tasted great."

"That makes sense then. He is showing me that he loves watching over you while you cook. It makes him happy."

"What? Really? But why can't I see him? I would love to see him. I wouldn't freak, I promise."

"He says that it isn't because he doesn't want to, but he says it is painful. Revealing oneself to the living. I get the sense that he was not happy he died where he did. Do you want tell me his name yet?"

"Not yet. I will, promise. It's just that I would like a bit more confirmation."

"Hmm...Okay. Well. I see blue sky and clouds. He is looking up and he is smiling. Was he in a helicopter?"

"Yes. He was medevac'd to the city. He was all alone as there wasn't any room to be with him in the helicopter. We were going to head up there in the morning and that's when we got the call that he had passed. I know he never wanted to be in the hospital. He had spent way too much time in them over the past several years. He was alone when he died and that is what has been bugging me all these years. That I couldn't be with him. And I suppose I just need him to know that I am sorry I wasn't there."

"Olivia. I know you are sad, but he says that he wasn't alone. That he had family with him the entire time. That he understands why you weren't there, but also, he never wanted you to see him like that. He is at peace now and he needs you to know that."

As I passed her the Kleenex, my little spirit friend showed me my uncle!

"Oh my goodness! Olivia, he just showed me my uncle Carl! Why would he know my uncle?"

Smiling, Olivia replied, "Because he did know your uncle. They played darts and pool together all the time. He really liked your uncle."

"Okay, you have to tell me what his name is!"

"It is Robert. He knew many of your family members. It is a small community after all," laughed Olivia.

"Wow. Okay. That is such a surprise. There seems to be a spirit trying to push through, but I am going to make her wait. Your brother is telling me that there is going to be a baby. And that this baby is going to be infatuated with cars. Anything that has an engine actually. He says to encourage it and teach him all about them."

"But there isn't anyone having a baby. Maybe it is his grandson? When he passed his daughter-in-law was pregnant."

"I am not sure. He just says there is going to be a baby boy. When a spirit shows me something you may not understand what it means until a later date. And spirits don't have a sense of time. We know that it has been say 5 years, but to them they do not understand that. To them it may feel like 5 minutes. So when something is revealed it may be weeks, months or even years until you understand what it meant."

"Okay. That is interesting."

"It is. And when we rely on time every day of our life, it may be hard to wait for the vison to reveal what it means. But it will come. Being patient is something I myself have a hard time with."

CHAPTER 8

"Did your brother walk with a cane? I get the sense that he had to use one."

"Yes. Toward the end he needed one for balance. Why?"

"Well, I see he isn't using it very much anymore. His body is healing."

"You can see him? Actually see his face?"

"No. I see the essence, the light of him. He is giving me the impressions of what he wants me to see and reveal to you."

"Oh. But he is okay. He has no more pain?"

"Yes he is okay. Do you have two brothers? He is showing me a brother."

"No, I had only one brother."

"Hmmm… Well he is showing me his brother. Another man. You're sure?"

"Very. Can he maybe describe him to you? I may be able to figure out who he wants me to see."

"I get the feeling that he loved and respected this man. Robert says that he is about his height but heavier. Balding and has a little bit of a belly and…

"Oh my!" Said Jen, Olivia's friend, as she almost fell out of her chair.

"Wow!" Replied Olivia.

"Who is it? You must know as you both seem shocked."

"He is describing my husband. But why? My husband isn't dead."

"He just wants you to know that he loved and respected your husband tremendously. He loved him because he loves and takes such good care of you."

"His brother-in-law. He considered my husband his brother. That makes me so happy. And he is going to make me cry again," sighed Olivia.

"He is ready to go. Do you have anything else to ask him?"

"He truly is okay now?"

"Yes. He is where he is supposed to be. He says he loves you."

"Then no. I have no more questions for him. Just tell him that I love and truly miss him."

"He can hear you. But he says good-bye. Wow. That was interesting. I can't believe he knew my uncle. Such a small world. Well, you have lots of time left. Do you have any more questions? I have a lady here that has been not so patiently trying to push her way through. But I have kept her waiting. Do you want me to go ahead?"

"Sure. This is all so very interesting to me. I wonder who could want to talk with me."

"Well there is two different ladies actually. But this particular one is somewhat pushy. So we will start with her. She is telling me that she wants to thank you for helping take care of her."

"Oh… Is it my grandmother or my aunt? They are the only ladies that I know of that have passed away."

"No. She is now laughing at a memory she is showing me. She says that when she got married it was like and inside joke with her friends that her husband was marrying an M & M."

"Like the candy?"

"I suppose. But I am getting the impression it is about initials. She is showing me friends all gathered together celebrating. It was a happy time in her life."

"Grandma Marian, my husband's grandmother is the only other lady that I helped take care of. And it wasn't that much. We were always so busy. But I was glad to help any time that she needed me."

"She just wanted to say thank you. That she appreciated everything you did for her. That she is sorry she was cranky. I get the feeling she didn't want to be wherever she was. But she never got the chance to say that to you. And now she is gone."

"She was always like that, laughed Olivia. Always on the run. Never slowing down. She was a nice woman but you are right she didn't want to be moved from her home."

"Now this other lady, she loves you dearly and wanted you to know that. And to apologize for her attitude at the end. She is telling me that wasn't who she was."

"That has to be my Aunt Sarin. She can hear me?"

"Yes. Spirits can hear and see us. You just can't hear or see them," replied Charlene.

"Oh aunty. You were sick. I completely understood that your health made you say and do things that you wouldn't ordinarily do. I love you too. I don't blame you for anything."

"She is talking about someone. Very adamant that we get her a message. Does she have children?"

"Yes. Two girls. One is a teacher and the other has health issues."

"That one. The girl with health issues. She needs you to tell her that if she does not straighten out soon and figure things out, that her health will fail and her life will be no more."

"Oh goodness. Yes! Yes, I will definitely get her the message."

"That is all she wanted. She is fading and gone now. You have a little more time. Do you have any other questions?"

"I do. My granddaughter seems to keep having some horrible dreams. And I don't understand why. They are very real to her and she is afraid to go into rooms by herself or even to just go to sleep. Is there anything we can do to help her?"

"Well, let's ask Spirit. What is her name?"

"Shaylynn. She is only six years old. And I just want to help her have a peaceful nights rest."

As I said her name and asked Spirit to show me what was plaguing this young child, they released to me something that Olivia was going to be very shocked over.

CHAPTER 9

"You are going to either be shocked or not by what I am going to tell you. Spirit has revealed to me that your granddaughter has a nasty little ghost hanging around and just likes to scare her. Like he gets the pleasure out of causing her stress."

"Oh. Well that is disturbing. I need to tell you that Shaylynn has seen and even talked to spirits or ghosts since she was about two years old. I just didn't realize that it could be a ghost that has been causing the dreams. Why? She is just a child."

"I can see that her dreams are very explicit. That they involve her mom?"

"Yes! She is always saying that they are trying to hurt her mom. And she can give you details. Like exactly where they are, what they say, it is very unsettling. I feel so awful for her. Is a ghost and spirit the same thing? Is it trying to hurt her?"

"No. It just wants to bug her. There is a difference between the two. A spirit is a soul who does not seek to harm anyone. They generally are around to make sure their loved ones are okay. And also to let their family know that they too are alright. Spirits have a purpose for being here, generally they have a message for someone. A ghost on the other hand, is usually someone that has died a horrific death. They are lost and angry. They don't understand what has happened. They have no purpose for being around. So they tend to cause mischief. And once again to the spirit and ghosts, there is no timeline. They could have died ten years ago but to them it feels like the present. This is why when they reveal to me that something is going to happen, we don't know if it's going to be ten minutes, ten days or ten years. They just know that it will."

"Wow! That is a lot to take in. But is there anything that we can do to help Shaylynn? Any way of getting rid of this ghost?"

"What Spirit is telling me, is for you to get some sage and burn it around every window and doorway in the house while saying a little prayer. Also, if you can get some pink Himalayan salt I will give you a little bottle of Holy water. Put some salt in your hand and spritz it with the Holy water and sprinkle it in all four corners of her bedroom and over the doorway. Let this ghost know he is not welcome. This should help her tremendously."

"Oh thank you so much. I wasn't sure if I would believe you. Sorry about that. But you have helped me and by helping me you are helping Shaylynn, too. I can see you are such a blessing to so many people. Again, thank you."

"It is my pleasure. And don't worry Olivia. Many people have trouble believing in the spirit world. I hope that you got what you were looking for. And Olivia? I believe that your granddaughter has the gift. I see it in her and Spirit has shown me too. I would love to do a session with her if it would be okay."

"I would have to ask my daughter. I will let you know. So you think she is psychic?"

"Most assuredly she has a gift. I don't really know what kind. I am very interested in meeting your daughter too."

"Is there something you aren't telling me?"

"I really feel that your daughter and granddaughter both have a gift. I will need to meet them to be sure. This is crazy amazing if I am right. And I am usually not wrong about these types of things."

"I am stunned! Both of them? That is wild. I sure have a lot to think about. I am for sure going to get them here to meet you. I hope your day goes good for you. I know that you have made mine. Good-bye Charlene."

"Good-bye Olivia. I really enjoyed meeting you and discovering that your brother knew my uncle. Have a blessed day and drive safe." Phew! That was a long hour. "You can come out of hiding Jake. I know you snuck in the back door. Do you want to go throw a stick? I have some time before my next client."

"Ruff! Ruff!"

"Let's go! Race you to the yard! Hey! You cheater. I am going to get you for that!"

CHAPTER 10

It has been 2 weeks since I met Olivia. It's another beautiful day. As I sit on my front porch watching the sun make its appearance, I am pondering the pictures swirling around in my head. All these dreams that I have been having lately. Alice is still on my mind and now I have been having some odd and unsettling to say the least, visions/dreams. I think vision because I have not yet figured them out. At times I can determine what a dream means. But, for the last week my rest has been plagued by some very disturbing scenes. Hence is why I am up before the rooster! Because truly any normal person would be sleeping still, not getting up before the dawn of a new day. So with coffee in hand, I am trying to understand exactly what it is I am seeing. I so enjoy my sleep. I am not exactly a morning person, though I have been working on that. My unique ability brings me all kinds of information. Just usually not so troublesome.

Since these visions/dreams started, my mind just doesn't want to shut down. It feels like it is on some kind of speed! Running nonstop like an old movie reel. And none of it is making sense, yet. So here I am trying to put it all together. Kind of like a puzzle. Rearranging the scenes to put them in the correct order. The only part that I am not really sure about, is if it's from the past or if it is happening now. My "Spidey" radar, which is what my bestie calls it, is giving me the feeling that it is in the present. And I have this uncanny sense that I can feel another presence. Not just a soul that has passed, but someone alive! A person that may be feeding me all these things going on. And if that is the case, I need to figure this out ASAP! Many times in my life, I have had visions of the past. Usually, I see things that once was. I don't have the ability to talk to another, unless this person is a spirit. The gift of talking to another without words, is called Telepathy. I have been gifted with something special, but I have yet to try out telepathy.

Beep....Beep....Beep!

Crud! I have been sitting here awhile. The alarm is going off which means it is time to start my day. Monday is my day to do all the bills and make more teas, candles and holy water. I really enjoy the repetition of creating and of course the smells. The Angel Campaign is also a small retail store that sells these things to help others heal spiritually and to ward off those unruly ghosts or spirits that just won't leave someone alone. But first, the dreaded running. "Jake! Let's go boy. Time to get in the exercise."

"Ruff! Ruff!"

"You ready boy?"

"Ruff!"

"Okay. I guess I am too. Let's go!"

Jake is such a great listener and companion. I can just chat and run all my thoughts by him and he doesn't mind. I am so glad I listened to my Spirit guide when he told me that Jake was for me. I never have had a pet as I travel. But, this was the best decision and I am glad I didn't waiver on this. He is an irreplaceable friend and guide. He keeps me safe wherever we travel and as we run.

"Come on boy. We need to get the 3 miles in as today is work day in the kitchen. I have been trying different scents for candles and I think they will smell great. But of course we will use Alice as the tester first." Jake gives me a nudge when I need to pay attention, because sometimes my mind starts to wander.

"So Jake, what do you think about having Lucy over next month for a little while? You guys get along great already, and Alice and I are wanting those babies. Do you think you can handle her being in your space for a while?"

"Arrrruff!"

"Ha-ha! Oh yes, I think you won't mind at all. Okay boy. It is set. We will discuss everything with Alice later today. Okay big guy. Let's push it hard this last bit. I am anxious to get started on the new candles."

As we were rounding the final corner to the home stretch, I nearly fell to my knees when I was hit with a vison.

CHAPTER 11

My heart started racing. My hands were clammy and my vision started to fade. My entire body felt like it was encased in ice, I was shaking so bad. The sweaty hands and heart beating over time could have been from running, but I knew differently. I was getting a vision. What I saw and felt, because it did feel like I was there living this nightmare, made my blood run cold! Never have I ever had something like this happen. I could actually see around me and hear things I didn't want to bear witness to. When I looked around, it was dark and dreary with poor lighting. I saw hands that were dainty with light red hair running up an arm and a splattering of freckles. I realized at that very moment that what I was seeing, was from another person! A little girl or young woman. Not too old, maybe 12-14 years of age. And I/she was being held prisoner!

As my heart began to slow, and the vision started to clear, I took a couple of deep cleansing breaths to calm myself. Jake was right there, holding me up just about. As I was down on my knees now and freezing. "Good boy Jake. Good boy. Come on, we need to get home and call Alice. Thank you for watching out for me."

"Ruff, ruff!"

Alice is my best friend and confidant of the human kind. Jake doesn't mind sharing. He adores Alice and the feeling is mutual. Alice understands me and helps me sometimes get a different perspective on visions that I don't always have a clear idea of what or why it is happening.

"Alice? It's me. Please when you get this message call me back. It is important. I really need to talk to you. Call me."

Alice. Where would I be without her? She has always been there for me. High School would have been horrible without her there. Having someone watch your back and stick up for you, it is a feeling like none other. Alice is now a homicide detective and I couldn't be more proud of her. She is super smart and has a voice that could have made her lots of money. But she chose to protect and serve. She has never doubted my abilities and I sometimes help her on cases. Quietly of course. We both live just outside the city, where the air is pure and crisp. I have a view of the mountains and no neighbors close enough to see. Alice is another sounding board when I need it. Someone to vent to or discuss things with. Hopefully, she can help me with this vision. I have this horrible feeling that time is of the essence.

CHAPTER 12

"Good boy Jake. I am so glad you were there to protect our girl. Oh my goodness Charlene! What would have happened if Jake wasn't with you? You could have walked into the street! Or who knows what else would have happened."

"I am okay Alice. Now quit spoiling him. He did what he was trained for. And he is always with me. Now, how is our girl doing? I figure she will be coming into heat next month? Jake and I have discussed it and we think you should bring her out to stay with us for that month. Just to make sure that everything works out. What do you think?"

"I think you need to quit stalling and tell me what it is you called so frantic about. What happened in your vision that has you so visibly upset?"

"Okay, okay. I have been having some very unpleasant dreams. Pretty jumbled. I have been trying to figure them out. I just wasn't sure if they were from the past or now. But, after having the vision while running, I really believe they are in the now. This vision nearly had me on my knees Alice. Well, when I came out of it, I actually was on my knees. But Jake did what he was supposed to do. He was standing guard. Anyways, I know this vision has something to do with my dreams. What I saw…it made my blood run cold."

"What is it Charlene? What exactly did you see?"

"I saw a young girl. She, well, I got the feeling she was no more than maybe 14 or 15 years old. And I could hear things that sounded like others crying. I couldn't see too much as it looked dark and dingy. Like the lighting wasn't very good. But I could see my or rather her arm. It was dainty and had red hair and freckles all over it with a crescent shaped birthmark on her forearm. The sense that I was in a cage and trapped with no way out was imminent. I got this feeling she is hurting, scared and that someone is doing unthinkable things to her. But not just her. There are others too. I really feel she is losing the battle. Like she wants to give up. We have to do something Alice!"

I didn't realize I was crying, until Alice passed me the Kleenex box and a shot of whiskey. Jake had picked up on my distress and was pushing up against me. I reached down to pet him and reassure him I was okay. As I looked up at Alice, I could see the concern in her eyes.

"Thank you for the whiskey. What are we going to do? I truly believe that someone has kidnapped this young girl and possibly others."

"I am sorry honey. It has been awhile since you have had something of this caliber. But I don't think I have ever seen you this visibly upset. Not that the others weren't bad, but I truly have never seen you like this before. What is different about this one?"

"It felt like I was the one there Alice. It was like I could feel and hear everything that has happened to her. This is something new for me, so I really didn't get a handle on it before the vision went away. I don't know if they will return or if that is all I am going to get. But what I do feel, is that she is looking for a way out. And I don't mean physically escaping. She is thinking about ending her life somehow. We can't let that happen! We just can't."

"We won't sweetie. I am heading in now and I will run a missing persons in 3 towns every direction and states if I have to. If anything comes up, I will let you know right away. We will find her Charlene. If you get anything else and I mean anything, you call me immediately. Love you much my friend. I promise we will figure this out."

"Love you much, too my friend. Drive safe. And thank you Alice."

"Always, you know that."

As soon as Alice left, I headed out to my office and the kitchen that I make my products. Having busy hands will help me to not dwell on what I cannot change. I truly love to make candles and blending tea is an art I enjoy.

"Ring…ring…ring…"

"Hello, Angel Campaign. How can I help you?"

"Hi Charlene, this is Jean. I was wondering if it is possible to come out and talk with you. I know that you are usually closed on Monday. But it is very important or I wouldn't have called."

"Well of course Jean. I can make some time in about an hour. Will that work?"

"Yes! Thank you so much! An hour then. Bye."

"Bye Jean. Drive safely."

"Well Jake, I wonder what is bothering Jean. I guess we shall find out soon enough." I let my mind wander, thinking about the garden that Jake so graciously weeded out for me, while I finished up with the tea. Trying to focus on something else will take my mind off the horrible things that I saw today in my vision. And I need to clear my mind for Jean. As I finished the teas and started the kettle because Jean loves my tea, for some reason I felt I needed 3 mugs, so I took down 3 mugs. Not sure why but time will show me. Just about the time I put everything together, I heard the car pull up. And that was Jake's cue to head out back.

"Hi Jean. So nice to see you again. Please come on in."

"Hello Charlene. Nice to see you too. Thank you for seeing me today. I have a friend with me and that is actually why I called. This is my dearest friend Annie. Annie, this is Charlene, the one I told you about."

As I looked up to say hi to Annie and shake her hand, my heart stuttered. There was something about her. Like I should know her. I stared at her for a minute trying to sort out these feelings.

"Nice to meet you Annie. Won't you please come in? Jean the tea is ready, I just need to go get it from the kitchen. Why don't you show Annie into the sitting room and I will be right back." I smiled to myself because now I knew why I took down 3 mugs.

CHAPTER 13

"Well Jean, Annie. What can I do for you two today. From the phone call, I gather it is rather urgent?"

"Yes it is. Thank you again Charlene for seeing us. Annie is my dearest friend. She lives 3 towns south of us. She has been worried and at a loss as what to do so she called me. I instantly thought of you as you have helped me so much. So I suggested coming to see you. I am not positive if you will be able to help us at all, but it is worth a try."

I turned to Annie to let her know that I will try my best. And that same feeling was there. Why did I feel as if I should know her? Her aura….well I could see that something had her very upset.

"Annie. It is very nice to make your acquaintance. How can I help you today?"

Smiling her encouragement Jean held Annie's hand.

"I…I don't know where to start."

"Do you like tea? I have just blended this new one today and need to try it out. If you do not like it I can get you something different.

"Yes. Thank you. I am a bit nervous. Please accept my apology."

"There is no need for an apology. You take your time thinking it over while you sip your tea. I am not in any hurry."

As Annie gathered her courage, I kept getting the feeling of urgency. Why? I don't know but something is surely bugging Jean and Annie. Something of great importance. Something about Annie had my heart rate up. I just wasn't sure what the connection was yet, but it was there.

"Okay. I think I can talk now."

"Alright. Did you need to speak to a loved one? Have questions about your life direction?"

"No. No. Nothing like that. You see, my family, well my husband doesn't believe in anything like this. And so coming here was hard for me. I don't like going against his wishes. But I have become desperate! I don't have anyone but Jean to help me or even believe me!" cried Annie.

"Oh Annie. I will try to help you. But if this is so very important and urgent why me and not the police? Surely you can get help from them."

"I have tried! We have tried, Jean and me. My husband is the mayor of our town. He doesn't believe in someone like you. My parents are gone and I am an only child. So I have no one else to turn to. I have exhausted myself trying to get people to believe me!"

"Believe you? What is it that you are needing from me Annie?"

"My daughter is missing. She has been gone now for over 2 weeks! I have gone to the police and put posters up. But to no avail. My husband, he is not my daughter's real dad. They don't exactly get along and we don't have any other children just her. She means everything to me! This is not like her. She would never, never run away. I know it," sobbed Annie.

"Oh Annie! Your daughter is missing? And the police won't help you? But why?"

"Because we live in a small town. My husband is the mayor of our town. He is good friends with the Sherriff. I have tried to tell him this isn't like her but he doesn't believe me. They have never gotten along very well. She is head strong I know, but lately she has been very defiant toward him. She and I have a fantastic relationship. My husband told the police she ran away and that he feels when she is ready to go by his rules she will return. But Charlene, 2 weeks! And not a word from her. She would have called me."

"Have you talked to any of her friends? When was the last time you spoke or saw her?"

"She came home Friday after track practice. She has been in a weird mood for a while. But I just thought it was school or boys. She always used to talk to me. Never has she kept anything from me. But I could not get her to tell me what was wrong. She would always tell me when something was bugging her or if she got a weird feeling. But we had to always talk about that kind of stuff in private as my husband forbids us to discuss anything of that nature. She has always got these feelings when something was…"

"What kind of feelings Annie?" My heart just jumped. It started beating faster as whatever Annie was about to reveal was of gigantic importance. Annie just stared at me. I could see she was torn. And I wanted to ask her something, but just then I felt myself fading! I was about to have a vision and in front of a client! Ever since Annie walked through my door, I knew that something huge was about to happen. I can't remember there being a time when I have been so anxious.

CHAPTER 14

As I faded into my vision I could hear sounds around me. I smelled mustiness, stale food and unwashed bodies. My wrists hurt like they had been pulled over my head and left like that. Everything was hazy. I could barely open my eyes. Almost like I had been drugged. But I was attempting to look around. The pain! Oh I hurt everywhere. I could hear voices. Not out loud but in my mind. Like someone or more than one person was surrounding me. Trying to encourage me to hang on, don't give up. Then I heard a door opening. The sound grated on my nerves and my heart started pounding! The door opening meant that he was coming! God no! Please not again. I can't do this again!

When I attempted to open my eyes and look around all I could see was a shadow coming closer. He was big that much I could determine. As he drew closer I realized that he was wearing a mask or a hood of some kind to disguise his features. He walked right up to me and pulled my chin up to look at him.

"I want my mom! Momma! Please help me! Why? Why are you doing this?"

"No one can help or hear you Lara. No help is coming

to take you out of here. You are ours and always will be until we say otherwise."

"No! No! No!"

"Charlene! Charlene! Come on honey please come back to us. That's it. Here sip on this, it will help to calm you. Oh sweet mercy! What happened to you? What did you see? You were talking like you were someone else and then you just started screaming!"

"I am so sorry that you two had to witness that. Thank you for the tea. Can you give me a few minutes please? I just need to breath and think about this vision. I promise I will continue Annie."

"Of course! We can leave and do this another day if that's what you need," said Jean.

"No. Please I just need to think about this for a moment. I am pretty sure this involves you or rather Annie."

As I looked up and across the settee toward Annie, I could see she was as white as a ghost. No pun intended. She was shaking so badly she could barely hold her cup of tea. I am pretty sure my visions of Lara, is the same young girl that Annie is here about. And I know I am not telepathic so that means that Lara must be. And how she found me, I am not sure at all. I really need Alice to get here as soon as possible.

"I need to call my friend. She is a detective and I know she will help us."

I turned to Annie and just looked at her. I now knew what that connection was. Annie had beautiful green eyes and deep auburn hair. And when she raised her hand up to take a drink, I saw a familiar crescent shape birthmark on her wrist.

"Annie. Your daughter Lara didn't run away. You are

very much correct about that. She has been kidnapped. Why didn't you tell me that Lara was gifted?"

Annie took some deep breaths and set down the beautiful china. How and what did she tell Charlene? Not even Jean was aware of Lara's abilities. No one but she and her husband. "I didn't tell you her name. How did you know what it was?"

"I heard her name spoken. She has red hair about your color, green eyes and is around the age of 14. She runs because it helps to clear her mind. And she has a crescent shaped birthmark just like yours, but on her hand. I know, because she has been sending me visions while I was sleeping for over a week. I have not been able to make sense of them, as they were just clips of some very disturbing things. But now I understand why I felt a connection to you when you walked into the office. She has somehow connected with me. She doesn't talk to me. It's like I am there. I feel, see and hear everything she is doing."

"Please! Tell me if she is okay!"

"Honestly I don't know. I do know she is alive. I feel she is hurt, but I don't know how badly. I know she is somewhere damp and musty. The lighting is very dim, but it was enough to see things. I really need to get my friend here and get her involved. We must hurry on this."

"No! You don't understand. My husband is not going to be okay with this. He won't believe any of it. He will be very angry that I sought you out", cried Annie.

"Annie, please let her help, begged Jean. We need the police. They can now start looking in earnest. Why didn't you tell me that Lara was like Charlene?" asked Jean in a hurt voice.

"Oh Jean, please don't be angry with me. I have always wanted to confide in you. But since I married Johnathon, I have had to keep it secret. He forbade me to ever speak of it to anyone. I didn't really know that Lara could talk to others or hear what they were thinking until she was about 6 years old. It just came out one night when we were sitting down to dinner. She corrected him on a story he was telling. She told him that he was lying. It was not a good night at all. He demanded that she tell him what she thought she knew. So she did. She told him that his mother whom had passed away over 10 years prior to us marrying, told her the story and she said that he was lying. Lara is a very honest person. She would never tell an untruth, but Johnathon insisted she was and she was punished! From that night on, I had her promise that she would never speak of anything like this in front of him. That she could tell me when Johnathon wasn't around. It would be our secret. And we never did talk about anything that she told me, in front of him. And Charlene, she always told me everything. But lately she has been very distant and not saying much. I could tell that something was truly bugging her. I need my baby back!"

Annie was in a full melt down at this point. Me? I was feeling sick and very pissed off! How dare him! I needed some air. So I told Jean to take care of Annie and I would return as soon as I called my friend. We needed to put our heads together and find this sweet girl. As I walked out and over to my flower garden, I tried to piece together everything Lara was trying to show me. And I called Alice to let her know what happened. She promised that she would be there as soon as she possibly could.

CHAPTER 15

It took Alice about an hour before she made it to my place. And of course Jake greeted her enthusiastically. Jake had been sitting close to Annie and giving her comfort, although she didn't even realize it.

"Charlene. What is going on?" asked Alice

"Well good news and bad. Which do you want first?"

"Good first. You know that."

"Okay. I have figured out what my dreams are about and who they are about. That's the good news. And I was right. That is the bad news."

"You being right is bad?" asked Alice with a smirk.

"Remember when I told you that I felt this young girl was being hurt? Well that is true and I know this because she has somehow connected with me. And I….

"Wait! She has connected with you? As in she is talking to you? That is great! We can just ask…

"No, she doesn't talk to me. I don't even know if she realizes that in her state of distress she has reached and found me. But she has and here is the weird thing. When I had my last vision, which by the way was embarrassing to have in front of a client, I could hear voices all around me/

her. They were telling her to not give up. But I didn't see anyone. What I felt and heard was spirits. Like I feel when I am doing a reading or meditating."

"Holy cannoli Bat-man! Are you telling me this young girl is just like you? She can hear spirits too?" asked Alice.

"Yes. Yes she can." Said Annie as she walked up behind us. Neither of us had heard Jean and Annie come out of the house.

"Annie. This is my best friend and homicide detective Alice Beaumont. She is here to help you. And yes Annie, she does believe in what I can do. She knows how to help without bringing undue attention to me and my clients. Please just give her a chance. Tell her everything and let her do what she does best."

"Are you sure? Because my husband has our sheriff's department convinced she has run away."

"Annie, hi. I am Detective Alice Beaumont. Please let's go sit and discuss everything. You said you hung up posters of Lara right? Well we will just hang them here and all over every town that is near you. No one will suspect anything. They will just see a very distraught mother looking for her child and hanging up more posters. If it was my child I would be doing the same thing. So please, come in and talk with me. Let me try and help. If we have any trouble with your husband I will deal with him."

"Okay. But Johnathon thinks that Jean and I are at lunch. I really need to be home before him."

"I promise you Annie, we will be done and have you back on the road very soon." Said Alice

When Jean and Annie left, Alice reached for her phone to call the precinct. She asked her friend to send the picture of Lara to every department in every police and Sherriff station for a 100 miles in all directions.

"I cannot believe that jackass Sherriff did not send Lara's photo to other stations! What the hell was he thinking? That just because he is friends with the mayor he didn't have too? Runaway or not she is a minor, a child out there all alone. You better believe when I say he is going to answer for that, means he is going to pay. I am going to have my friend at the FBI look into him! I am going to…

"Here, take this and breathe." I handed her a shot of whiskey. A small one, knowing she was heading back to work shortly but needing a little calming. I took one myself, as this day wasn't over and poor Lara was out there all alone and scared, possibly hurt badly.

"Okay, I needed that. Thank you. I am going back to the precinct and do some checking up on this piece of work called a Sherriff. I pray that someone has responded to our amber alert! You just focus and see if anything else comes through or maybe Lara will connect again. And keep this loving, slobbery mutt with you at all times. He seems to pick up on things out of sort. Don't you boy? Be safe Charlene and please let me know if you have any more contact with Lara."

"I will. And you be safe, too. You will let me know if you find out anything."

"You know I will."

When Alice hugged me good-bye and left, I was putting the closed sign up and going to do some serious meditating. Maybe, just maybe, Spirit will be able to help me connect with Lara. I set fire to my favorite scented candles and pulled out my meditation mat. As I started my deep breathing, I concentrated solely on Lara. I opened my mind like never before, reaching for her. I could feel myself starting to drift and I knew that Spirit was there. I reached for the tarot cards I always have nearby. The most important thing is finding and connecting with Lara. From what I learned from Annie, I knew that Lara was a very special girl. She had a powerful gift of speaking to the spirits, but I think that there may be even more to her gift. As I picked up my cards and started to turn them over, I had a sense of urgency! I did not feel Lara, but when I looked down at what Spirit had me lay out, my heart skipped a beat, maybe even two.

Something was very, very wrong. And poor Lara was in horrible trouble. But not just her. If I read the cards correctly, there seems to be more young girls involved! I felt so cold inside. How could anyone do something so horrific to a child? I needed to call Alice right away! But as I stood to go get my phone, two things happened at once. I saw Jake lunge towards me and I was hit with a vision.

CHAPTER 16

A ll I could make out was a haze. I felt drugged again. The smells I was picking up made me want to vomit. I heard someone crying and moaning in pain. I wasn't sure if it was Lara that I heard and smelled or someone else.

"Lara? Lara honey can you hear me? Please Lara, my name is Charlene. I don't know if you realize it, but you have connected to me somehow. Can you hear me? Try Lara! Come on sweetheart try to talk to me. I have never done this so I need you to help me."

I really didn't know if it would work, but I had to try. I have never spoken telepathically to anyone. Then again I have never tried before either. But Spirit was with me and I know they were with Lara, too. If nothing else, the haze was lifting. I could make out things a little better. I felt so cold and my body hurt. I looked around and saw the most horrific sight! There in front of my eyes were so many cages. All numbered and with a young girl in each one! My stomach turned at an alarming rate. I knew I was going to be sick. What in the name of all that is holy was I seeing? Who would do this to these precious babies? Where were they? Was it a sex ring or kiddy porn operation? Just then, I heard a door screech open. My heart rate jumped! I started to shake as I watched the same masked man walk towards me. All I could feel was fear!

"Lara! Lara please hear me! Damn it Lord I need her to hear me! Please!"

"Good afternoon Lara. I hear you gave your master some trouble today? I have told you over and over if you will just give us what we want, you wouldn't be hurt."

"I hear you," whispered Lara.

"I know you hear me witch! Look at me when I talk to you! Are you ready to behave? Or do you need another lesson?"

Oh my God! "Lara? You can hear me can't you?"

"Yes," came a small whisper.

"Okay baby. I need you to tell me if you know who took you or where you are?"

"Yes? Yes what? You ready to behave or you want another lesson? Well? What is it going to be? Look at me when I am talking to you," spoke the man.

"No." answered Lara. "No, I don't want a lesson and no I will not behave. I have done nothing wrong. I do not know who you are or why or where you have taken me!"

"Listen you little witch! You are going to do as we say or you will be punished some more. And of course you don't know who I am. Why would you even say that?"

Suddenly he grabbed my chin, squeezing with such force, my teeth ground together. Forcing me to look up at him. I saw intense blue eyes. Almost to blue, like he was wearing contacts. And I smelled his strong aftershave. A very sickly, sweet scent. All I wanted to do was gag. And his breath smelled like cinnamon. I will never want cinnamon again. I just stared into eyes that showed true evil.

"Please Lara, don't make him hurt you. Just stay quiet. Look around if you can, show me as much of the place as possible. Blink sweetie if you understand."

As I waited, I got this feeling that I knew him. And then my eyes closed and opened. Well Lara's did.

"That's good Lara. Please just do as they want. We are trying desperately to find you. Your mom and my dearest friend. We have the police involved and I know now that you are not the only one."

"Well girl? You know what it is that your master wants from you. Are you ready to cooperate? Or do we need to take you back to the room?"

As I stared into those blue, evil eyes, I heard Lara answer, "G0 TO HELL!" And then the connection was gone.

When I came around, I found myself laying on the floor with Jake on my legs nudging me and whimpering.

"Oh Jake. Oh Jake we need to call Alice right away! Help me up boy, hurry! That's it. Thank you so much. You are the best my love."

Whatever is happening to Lara is specific. She is being tortured along with many others, but they want something particular from Lara. And from the sounds of it, she is strong willed and is not giving them whatever they have requested. She may be ready to throw in the towel, but she is not going to give them anything before she goes. Sweet mercy we need to figure this out and fast!

"Alice? Oh my God Alice you need to get here as soon as you can! I have had a doozy of a vision. It isn't pretty. We are up against not just a kid napping! Please hurry as soon as you get this message."

Well damn! She must be busy. All I got was her voice mail which is unusual. She always answers my phone calls.

"Well Jake, we need to get Jean and Annie back out here."

"Ruff!"

"I don't care what anyone says buddy. You are one heck of a partner. Give me a hug you lovable, big guy."

As I hugged my wonderful companion/partner, I flipped open my phone to dial Jean's number. We need everyone on board for this. And I need to let Annie know that I have spoken again to Lara.

CHAPTER 17

"Jean? This is Charlene. I haven't heard from Alice yet, but I really need to talk with Annie again. As soon as possible would be best."

"Oh Charlene! Is it bad? I don't think I can get her out there until tomorrow. She mentioned that Johnathon is leaving town for a few days. Will that be soon enough?"

"Yes. That is fine. And I will tell you all I know when I have Annie here."

"Can you just tell me if she is alive? Please?"

"Yes Jean. She is alive. Hurting. But alive. I will see you both tomorrow around 9 if you can."

"Okay, we will be there. Thank you Charlene. I am so glad I brought her to you."

"Me too Jean. Me too. Have a good evening."

I walked over to look down at the cards once more. And again I got goose bumps and felt nauseated. What in the world is happening with these poor girls? I had a bad feeling it was kiddy porn or a sex trafficking ring. Either way one was just as horrible as the other! What keeps nagging me? I need to pin it down. Was it something that the hooded man said? Or something I saw? I will figure it out. I have too.

"Charlene? Where are you girl?" Yelled Alice as she walked through the office.

"Back here Alice."

"Sweet baby Jesus! What is wrong? I got your message. And boy are you going to want to hear what I found out. Not sure if it has anything to do with Lara but…What? What is wrong honey?"

"Oh Alice! It is way worse than we thought. And yes, your news has everything to do with Lara."

"How do you know that? Never mind. Dumb question. Okay, what exactly did you see? I need to write all this down."

"Nothing good, that is for sure. But you are never going to believe what I have to say. I tried speaking to Lara. You know, telepathically. I needed for her to hear me. And guess what? She did! She talked to me!"

"Say what! Are you sure Charlene? This has never happened before."

"I know! But honestly Alice, I think that Lara is a medium like me but also a very strong telepathic. She may even be able to do other stuff. I don't know, but she heard and answered me."

"Wow! Just…wow. Well what did she say? What did you see? Does she know…?

"Slow down! Let's sit down over a shot of whiskey. I am not in the mood for wine tonight. This whole mess is just horrible. My nerves are shot. I didn't realize how long I was connected with her. I also called Jean and she is bringing Annie out tomorrow at 9 a.m. Will you stay tonight? Then you won't have to make an extra trip."

"Of course. Let me go get Lucy out of the car. You pour

and I will be right back. Then we will put our heads and notes together. We need to figure all this out and soon. We will call in reinforcements, too. I think we will be putting together a task force if this is as big as I believe it to be. I will return shortly. I just need to call my Captain and let him know I will be in later tomorrow."

I woke early. I don't think I slept a wink. I put on my running clothes and was getting ready to head out when Alice walked in.

"Please tell me you are not going out this early? The freaking sun isn't even up yet! I haven't had my coffee." Alice pouted.

"The timer is on and it will be ready for us when we get back. And I will make you some scones."

"What do you mean us? You know I hate running. How about I make the scones while you are out jarring all those bones together."

"Quit being a baby. You may not like running but it helps to clear the mind. And we need to have clear minds to figure out everything. So go get on some running shoes and wake those sleeping mongrels. They can come too."

"Flipping slave driver. I will come, but I am putting extra jam on my scone! Lucy! Jake! Get up you lazy dogs. If I am going then so are you two. Move it!"

Laughing at my friends antics made my morning. Alice may grumble, but she is in great physical shape. She works out all the time and she runs. Maybe on a treadmill, but she runs. And this is so much better than being cooped up inside a smelly gym any day.

As we started out, the dogs did their business and Alice and I chatted about mundane stuff. I don't mind talking while I run, but usually it is to Jake. Wasn't long and my mind started to drift. While I was pounding the pavement my mind was working overtime. Alice could sense that I was off in my own world and left me to it. She knows me well, and knew that when I figured it out, I would let her in on it. There is something bugging me still. Besides this whole fiasco, I feel like I am missing something. It is just hanging in the back of my memory. If only I could piece it together.

"What's up? You have this very determined look on your face. You remember something?"

"No. And that's just it. I know I am missing something. I can't seem to grasp it. Whatever it is, it's just out of my reach. I will remember."

"I know you will. I guess this fresh air stuff isn't half bad. Maybe I…Charlene? Hey boy, come here. Just stay with her. This is what happens Jake? Sweet mercy! Son of a bitch! She could get hit by a car or something. I am so glad you are with her. Okay boy, you just sit here and wait. I have to take this call. Captain? Yes, I am awake."

I am not sure what triggered the vision, but my guess is Lara. I am back in that horrible place, but this time I can see clearly.

CHAPTER 18

"Lara? Can you hear me?"

As I waited for her to acknowledge me, I could feel Jake standing guard. My heart was beating so fast. I knew something important was happening.

"Charlene? Can you hear me?" whispered Lara in my mind.

Oh Lord! "Yes Lara! Yes honey I can hear you. Can you look around a little more so I can see everything?"

"You have to hurry! They are moving the girls! Something is going on and they have decided to move everyone. I don't know what's happening, just that they are getting ready to move them. Please, you have to help us. Can you tell my mom that I love her? That I didn't give them what they wanted. I stayed strong."

"Lara! Give them what? Please just listen to me. Don't give up. And you can tell your mama as soon as you see her again. We are close, and we have many reinforcements to help us. Can you tell at all where you may be?"

"I can hear trains once in a while, and it smells funny. They have all the windows blacked out so that we can never see anything. Oh no! He is coming back!"

"Who Lara? Who is coming? Don't lose me honey. Just keep me with you. I know you can. Let me try and help you."

"Okay."

I watched whoever was under the hood walk to each cage and tell the girls to stand. It was obvious they had all been bathed and groomed. He handed them all a new dress to slip on. I tried real hard to study every minute detail that I could about the jailer. I needed to be able to give Alice as much information as I could. Then he walked over to Lara. The smell of cinnamon on his breath and the strong, over powering smell of his aftershave made me want to gag!

"Well sweet Lara. Soon it will be time to leave. You are going to a very special place. Not like the others, but just as nice. We can use your talents more than you know. We have gotten a very nice price for you."

"Lara? How do they know you have a special talent?"

"This is what I wouldn't give them. They have always known." whispered Lara in my mind.

"Okay Lara. We are looking for you. Please don't give up. And try to gather any clues as to where you are or may be going. Just stay strong! You can do this, I know you can. I am here anytime day or night."

"I need to go. They are gathering the numbers together. Please hurry Charlene!"

"Charlene? Hey girl. Come on now. It will be okay. Oh don't cry! You know I cry when you cry. Please take a couple deep breaths and tell me what happened."

"This is so wrong! My heart is breaking for all those girls. From what I can tell, they are all part of sex trafficking and kiddy porn. Except...

"Except what Charlene?"

"Except for Lara. They know Alice! They know she has a gift! And they are trying to use her to exploit it for some purpose. Each girl was in a numbered cage and they had a number pinned to their dress. They always called them by their numbers. Alice we have to….Oh My God! That's it! They called her by her given name! Not a number. But her name! They know who she is! Whoever has her, knows her personally! But how? And most importantly who?"

"I don't know but we are going to find out. Didn't Annie say that only her and her husband knew about Lara's talents? If that is the case then that narrows it down quite a lot, don't you think?"

"Yes it does. We need to hurry back. You need to get to the station and get whomever you can on board. I will give you all the details so you can pass them along. I can't stress how quickly everyone needs to move on this. They are moving the girls. I am not sure why, but somehow they must have gotten tipped off."

I jumped in the shower while Alice went off to the station. I put the kettle on and tried to hurry. But my emotions got the best of me and I lost it. At least no one can be witness to my red, blotchy eyes and puffy face. God I hate crying. Yes it's good for the soul, but good gosh what it does to your face! My heart is breaking for all these children. I am so angry, to the point of hate at those that are involved in something this disgusting. Why? What makes someone so evil? Why does God allow this? The whistle was blowing when I walked into the kitchen. I made my tea and went to my room. I needed some quiet and to collect myself before Lara's mom Annie and her friend Jean showed up. I bowed my head and prayed to God. I asked Him to forgive me for doubting Him. I know everything happens for a reason. We may never know what that is in our life time, but I know better than to question the why's of this life.

After my prayer, I closed my eyes and sought my Spirit guide. I went over everything I could remember and for whatever reason, Spirit kept bringing the smell of cinnamon to my mind. And the nasty smell of that aftershave. So I know this must be an important clue to the case. About the time I was done, I heard a car drive up. Must be Annie and Jean. I walked to the front room and greeted them as cheerfully as I could. "Ladies. Please come in. I just warmed up some water for tea. Would you like to join me?"

"Yes, thank you. Are you okay? Something happened didn't it?" asked Annie

"Yes, but this mess you see upon my face is just my emotions getting the best of me. Sometimes being so fair skinned has its disadvantages. I absolutely hate what crying does to me. Please sit, I will return and then we will talk."

As I was walking back into the living room, my phone started to ring. And since I have a special tone for Alice, I knew that's who was calling. "Hello. You got something already?"

"Hey girl. Has Jean and Annie arrived yet?"

"Yes, as a matter of fact they just arrived and we are getting ready to sit with some tea and discuss everything that I know. Why? What's up?"

"Well, go ahead and talk to them. I called to tell you that we have a task force assembled and that the captain is calling a meeting in 3 hours. There will be an officer from every station in a 100 mile radius, plus the FBI. I would like you to be here. I need your insight. I need to know if any of them are in anyway involved."

"You think that this whole thing is run by cops? Why would you think that?"

"I don't know that for sure. This is why I need you. But I do think something is up with the Sherriff from Annie's town. He never should have ignored this situation. Even if he is friends with the stinking mayor. And that is another person of interest. Her husband is a little hinky to me."

"Hinky?" I laughed because that has been Alice's new go to word for anything out of the ordinary. "Yes we will all be there. Is that alright?"

"Of course. Bring them. I want everyone to see that she is a grieving mother. And I want to know if a certain someone has a problem with her being there. I will see you all in 3 hours."

I turned to the ladies and found them wide eyed and staring intently at me.

"Well, it seems we are needed at the station. But first, let's talk about what I have found out so far. I will bring you up to date and then we will go to the police station. Alice seems to think I can be of use to her, and she wants all the officers to see that you are grieving for the loss of your daughter. That she isn't just a run away." We all sat down and I told both everything that had happened today and what Lara had to say. After we drove to the station and when we arrived there it was apparent we weren't the only invited guests. There was at least 15 sets of grieving parents inside the meeting room. I could feel so many emotions coming off them, it was a bit over whelming. All or most of the officers were standing around the edges of the room as the chairs were all taken.

"Oh my goodness! Charlene? Who are all these people?" asked Jean while she stared around the room.

"These are parents of young girls gone missing. Just like you Annie," I said while I watched her.

Annie sat down with a heavy heart. I could see that she was on the verge of crying. She looked all around her to see that she wasn't the only parent that has lost a child. Then her eyes landed on someone across the room. If she was pale before, she was downright white now. I followed her line of vision and saw a Sherriff and another gentleman staring at her. And now I know who her husband and his buddy the Sherriff were.

CHAPTER 19

"Annie? It's going to be okay. They were issued an invitation since this all started in your hometown. Just sit here with Jean and I will be back in a few minutes."

I walked over to where Alice was standing with her Captain. He was a very handsome man, with an aura that I wouldn't mind looking more into. But of course at a later date. He is extremely dedicated to his team and this town. I could tell that this was very disturbing to him. All these girls gone missing but not just from Lara's town. I wasn't sure how many departments were here. Why hasn't any of this come to light before? Well, it is out there now and I pray that we can find them before they are moved and scattered all over who knows where.

"Captain. I brought Annie with me. Are all these people missing someone?" I knew this but I wanted him to tell me.

"Yes, they all have someone missing. Some have been gone for a very long time. Others not so long. Who knows if they are part of this mess or not. But they all want answers and I will try and give them something today. I just pray that we find what the hell is going on before it's too late. Now if you will excuse me, I need to talk with the other officers before we get started. It was good seeing you again Charlene."

"It was good seeing you too." I watched him walk away. Who wouldn't? He had a very nice back side to look at.

"Okay Charlene, I would like you to just do whatever you need to do. We are looking for...I don't even know what. This whole thing is such a gigantic fubar! All we are going to do for now is up date everyone as much as we can and get all these parents that have someone missing's information and update it all. Thank you for being here. I can't tell you how much it means to have you helping."

"You never have to ask Alice. I will do everything I can. I am going to go back over to Annie. Her poor excuse for a husband is here and she is having a very hard time with it."

"Be careful around them. We really don't know anything about them yet. Stay with Annie."

As I approached Annie and Jean, I stopped short of saying anything. That smell! Where was it coming from? It was the same sickly sweet aftershave scent that Lara smelled. Sweet loving mercy, was the jailer here? Would he be so bold?

"Annie? Is this your husband?"

"Charlene! Annie said with panic-stricken eyes. Umm... Yes, this is my husband and Mayor of our town, Johnathon and this is Sherriff Adams. Gentleman this is Charlene Ensley. She is the one that has helped me get some help for Lara."

The scared but unwavering sound coming from Annie had me concerned. Was she afraid of her husband and this Sherriff? But once I looked into her eyes, I knew that she wasn't scared of them per say, and it wasn't really a frightened sound but an angry one. A determined one. She seemed to be stepping out of her shell and taking a stand against these two men whom didn't help the first time but now are at least acting like they are here for support. Way to go Annie. Stay strong.

"Gentlemen, it is nice to meet you." As I reached to shake their hand, it hit me. Cinnamon! Both of them smell like cinnamon. I felt sick. "If you will excuse me for a moment I need to use the restroom before we get started." I took my leave and as I walked through the room and toward the door I smelled the aftershave again. He was here! I need to get Alice's attention. I looked around and found her. She was staring right at me. She followed me out to the lobby.

"He is here! The jailer is here!" I bent over to take some deep breaths. The smell just hit me and made my stomach churn.

"What? Are you telling me that the man you saw in your vision is in that room? Hey are you okay?"

"Yes, yes and yes. I smelled the aftershave and the cinnamon. It just bombarded me and I feel nauseated. I will be okay. But Alice? I smelled the cinnamon on both Johnathon and the Sherriff. I don't know if they are involved, or they just both like cinnamon candy. Nevertheless, we can't overlook anything. As much as that will hurt Annie, we have to be sure. I just know that during my meditation, Spirit kept bringing back those two smells. He was telling me that it was important. I just didn't know why. I am afraid I do now."

"Okay. I need to think a moment. Do you know where you smelled the aftershave?"

"No. I just got a whiff of it. I don't know for sure whom

was wearing it. I honestly don't know if it's just a coincidence or if he would be so bold to show. It has to be an officer from one of the other towns. I only smelled the cinnamon on the Sherriff and Johnathon."

"I don't think anything you feel is a coincidence. You don't believe in coincidence. If you smelled the same scents, chances are whomever is involved is here so they can know what we are doing. I need to go and talk with my captain fast. We will decide what to say and not. Are you going to be okay?"

"I am. We really need to hurry. I am going to go sit with Jean and Annie. I will try and get a reading from others if I can."

We both returned to the room and as Alice walked up to her Captain, I went and sat next to Annie and Jean. The two men were not there but huddled together talking with another man.

"Okay you two. The meeting should be starting soon. Are you doing okay Annie?"

"Yes. Thank you. I didn't realize that there were so many families with children missing. I mean you hear about this type of thing on television and always think it would never happen to you. But it did. And my heart is breaking for all of us."

I let those two talk quietly while I did my deep breathing and let my mind reach out to Spirit. It wasn't going to be easy, as there were so many emotions flying around the room. But I concentrated on the group of 3 standing off in the corner chatting amongst themselves. The feeling I got from just those 3 were dark with a lot of anger thrown in. I must have been staring longer than I realized, because I felt a hand on my arm, shaking me.

"Charlene are you okay?" asked Jean.

When I looked up, to assure her that yes I was fine, my eyes landed on the other man that was talking with Johnathon and Sherriff Adams. I was looking into a set of eyes that were an intense color of blue!

CHAPTER 20

I have seen those eyes before. That was the jailer. Oh my! Why would he be here? Was he a police officer? Someone of importance? I really needed to find out and quick.

"Annie, without being obvious can you tell me who it is that your husband and Sherriff are talking with?"

"Sure." As she was talking with Jane, she casually glanced over. "I am not sure, but I think he is another Sherriff, can't be positive as I have never met him, I just know that he has been at meetings with others and my husband."

"Okay. Thank you. Well this meeting is about to get underway. Let's see what they have come up with."

As we listened to the Captain tell us everything they knew, I kept getting this feeling that someone was watching me. So when I looked around the room, I spotted ole fake blue eyes watching me. And me being me, I didn't want to let him think he could intimidate me, so I stared back. I didn't even blink. Yep, I won that one. I mean really, who does he thinks he is, trying to intimidate me. I was the champion in elementary school. No one could beat me at a staring contest. As the meeting was wrapping up, and questions were being tossed at the Captain, I noticed that the man with no name and the mayor left the meeting undetected. Well. At least I now have a face. Won't be long before we can put a name to it also.

"Ladies," Alice said as she walk up to us. "How are you holding up?"

"We are good, detective. Do you really think that this task force will be able to locate all these poor girls?" Asked Jean.

"We are going to try our best Jean. And Annie, please don't get discouraged. I will keep Charlene in the loop and she in turn will keep you posted. We got some great information from Lara, and I will use it to try and pinpoint where they may all be, I promise. Charlene? May I speak to you in private a moment?"

"Sure. Annie and Jean, I will talk to you both later. I promise to call if I get anything else."

"Of course. Did you see where my husband went?" asked Annie.

"I saw him leave just as the meeting was closing. He left with the other gentleman."

As I watched them walk out, I noticed that Sherriff Adams was also watching them. I didn't like the way he was looking at Annie. I turned to say something to Alice, when I felt or rather heard Lara. "Alice."

Alice looked at me and immediately knew that I was having a vision. But it wasn't really a vision as much as it was Lara talking to me. So she took me to the Captain's office, since it was private.

"Charlene? Can you hear me? Please, I really need to tell you something."

"Lara! Yes I can hear you. What is happening?"

"I….well, I heard them talking. The guards. We are leaving tonight! And they said something about a big truck. There is probably 20 of us girls here. So it has to be a fairly good size truck, right?"

"Yes it does. Lara, can you think of anything else? Something to help us locate where they are holding you?"

"I just know that when I was taken it wasn't a very long drive. And I can hear trains every now and then. I know we are being held downstairs. I counted 15 steps. It is dark and chilly. But only because the windows are all blacked out. I am sorry! I can't think of anything else."

"It's okay. That's great. Please hang in there. And if someone says anything else, you try and tell me. Okay? No matter what time it is."

"Yes, I will. Please hurry." And she was gone.

"Charlene? What happened? Did she say anything else?"

"Not really. Just that it wasn't a very long drive from where they took her. And that she counted 15 steps down once they were inside a building. And again the trains now and then. She said she overheard the guards talking that they were moving them out tonight. And something else about a big truck. Lara said she thought there were close to 20 of them. And that means they will need a truck large enough to put them all in."

"That is actually a great help. I know where she was taken, give or take a block or two. So we can do a search from there for trains. And we can look at all truck rentals and see if any has been rented for a short haul. This is something. Also, I have a few men that I trust completely. They are going to be tailing the husband, Sherriff and the man they were talking with. I didn't like the looks of him.

And no one recognized him either. But we have him on camera. Everyone in here has been captured on film. We will get a hit, I am sure of it. What is wrong?"

"That man? He was the jailer. I am positive. It's his eyes. They are the fake blue I saw in my vision. And I smelled the aftershave. Not sure who was wearing it, but I would bet, that he was the one. And another thing. Sherriff Adams is involved."

"Are you sure? 100% positive?"

"You know I wouldn't say anything if I wasn't. I honestly don't know how much Annie's stuck in the mud husband is involved, but I am more than positive that Sherriff Adams is. And the other guy? Annie said she had seen him at the house with others. All in a private meeting with the Mayor of course. But she has never been introduced."

"This sounds like it is bigger than we expected. If any law enforcement is involved that would explain why nothing was done or rather none of the girls were found. And sweet mercy how many towns? How far are they going to find these young women? And why would they bring the operation to such a small community? Why not hide in a big city?"

"All very good questions. Maybe because no one would ever think to look in such a small close knit communities. We may never find everyone involved, but we will get these people here. Those girls all need to be brought home. I pray we are fast enough to get them all."

CHAPTER 21

As I drove home my mind was thinking of any and all possibilities of where the girls could be. Lara is a brave young woman. I pray that her stepdad isn't involved, but at this point, it is looking like he and several others in police departments and who knows what other departments are behind it. They may not be the leaders, but they were up to their necks in what is happening. As I pulled into my yard and got out of the car, I got a very bad feeling. About then I heard Jake set up a ruckus. I need to get to Jake and let him out. He can run the perimeter and check for intruders. As I rounded the corner of my house where Jake is housed, I knew I wasn't alone. The hair on my arms and neck stood to attention. And then I smelled it.

"Well, well, well. If it isn't our little town physic, witch or whatever you call yourself. What were you doing at the meeting? You aren't a cop or any part of the task force."

I had my phone in my hand and I secretly hit Alice's number. "Pretty sure it isn't any of your business. So take a hike and get off my property before I let my dog out." As I turned to walk to the penned in area where Jake was seriously trying to jump over the fence, he grabbed my arm and whirled me around. As soon as he touched me I wanted to scream. The reading I was getting off him made me want to vomit. I could feel the excitement he was getting from squeezing my arm. "You have exactly 2 seconds to let me go or I will press charges for assault. And believe me, they will stick."

"Listen to me you little bitch! I am going to make your life a living hell if you don't back off from all of this. You don't want to mess with me."

"Do you know what happens when you push someone's fingertip in and down toward their hand?" I asked not really expecting an answer but I needed to distract him for a few more minutes. I knew that Alice would be flying to get here. "It sends out a sharp pain. It can bring a grown man to his knees." And right then I gave him a demonstration. "I asked you nicely to let go of my arm. No one touches me without my permission. My friend should be showing up real soon. You are one lucky individual Mr….

"I am not going to give you my name. And you better believe you will be seeing me again and real soon."

"I don't think so Mr. Pierce. I know plenty about you. But just to clarify something, I am not a witch. I am a physic/medium bitch and you are one perverted piece of shitake mushroom that will be going away for a very long time. Well, there is my friend and it looks like she brought some of her friends. But I think I will just keep you where you are for a few more minutes. Jake! Down boy. It's all okay now. Good boy. Good Boy Jake."

"Char! Are you okay? I got the S.O.S and came as fast as I could. Bill? Will you arrest this piece of shit? Read him his rights. We don't want any way for him to get out of this."

"Yes, ma'am. You have the right to remain silent. You have the….

"Well. You got here fast enough. Let me go get Jake before he rips the pen apart. But you best put that garbage inside the car first. We don't want him to sue me." Laughing I went to talk and calm down my sweet boy.

As the other police officers drove away, Alice came over to Jake and gave him a hug. Looked at me to make sure he didn't hurt me. "You pulled the old push the finger trick huh? You should have laid him flat on his ass. I know you can do it."

"I would have if that little trick didn't work. I am glad I put Jake in his pen. I would bet my last dollar he would have shot him."

"Well he didn't and I for one, am glad. But he could have shot you. What was he doing here? Did he say anything useful? Or did you get a reading off him?"

"Oh I got plenty from him. He is a very sick man that is for sure. He isn't the boss and I got names of most of the men in his employ. And best of all he is the one that rented the truck, so guess what his name is? And where it is going?"

"Give it up Charlene. You know I hate playing these games. I can get his name from finger prints."

"Baby. Okay his name is Devin Pierce. I am going inside to write down all the other names. And Alice? Johnathon is the one that gave them her name. Apparently she was getting to close to finding things out. All those babies are being used for kiddy porn. And when they out grow their usefulness they sell them off to the highest bidder. I am not sure if Johnathon told them about her gifts or they figured them out, but they were trying to use Lara for their own gains. I really need a drink of something, a shower and to call Jean and Annie. Not necessarily in that order."

"Thank you for this. And I am very glad you are okay. I need to go and get this wrapped up. It is going to be a long night. I will call you when I am done. Love you much my friend. Lock the doors."

"Yes sir!"

"Smart ass. I am being serious. There are others out there we need to gather before I feel you will be safe. Keep that bad boy with you and not in the pen tonight, please."

"I will and he always sleeps in the house. Love you much too my friend. Be safe." I locked the doors and windows then poured myself a two finger shot of whiskey and dialed Jean and Annie to give them the good news. I really hate not feeling safe, especially in my own space. But until all have been rounded up I will do as my bossy friend asked. Although, I have the best protector around.

As I laid down to go to what I was hoping would be a long restful sleep, my mind just wouldn't shut down. So, I got up grabbed my Bible and just let it fall open. When I looked down, it had opened to Psalm 23. As I read I was reminded that God is with me always. When I fell back to my pillow, I prayed to God and thanked Him for not only my safety but for my friends as well. I asked Him to watch and protect all those young girls. To bring them comfort and strength, because they were going to need it for a long time to come.

CHAPTER 22

The morning was beautiful. The sun was casting some fabulous colors against a partly cloudy sky. I haven't heard from Alice yet and don't expect to for the rest of the day. But I did get a call from Annie, crying with tears of joy that they found Lara and all the rest of the young ladies. They wanted to come out when Lara felt up to it. Of course I said yes! I want to hug Lara and let her know she is not alone in the gift department. Maybe I can help her adjust and learn what to do with her special talents. As I was watching the sun rise farther into the sky, I closed my eyes to meditate. I breathed in the fresh scent of pine and sweet peas. Yes those are my favorite and I have them planted everywhere. As I opened my mind, I got a visitor. She thanked me for helping find her granddaughter Lara and the rest of the children. I had quite a long conversation with Lara's grandmother and great grandmother. Apparently the gift runs in the family. How blessed Lara is to have such loving family to guide her.

"You ready for that run Jake? I need to get back and get us packed to head off to Montana. We have a group session in 3 days and I would like to have a day to do some serious meditating before I greet the group."

"Ruff!"

"Okay then. Let's get to it." I sure envy Jake. He doesn't have to stretch or worry about pulling a muscle. Wouldn't that be nice? Just get up and go with no worries. Well, since that is not going to happen, I better stretch extra good. No since testing fate.

Running is an evil way to exercise in my opinion. I don't particularly like it, but it does keep me in shape and helps the mind clear. I love meditating too, but this just gives me a little extra and Jake loves it. So running it is. I started thinking about my meeting in Montana. The advertisement should be in my email by the time I get back and I can check and be sure nothing needs to be changed. I usually get around 15 people sometimes more. And it is possible that if there are more than that I will stay and do another meeting. "Pick it up boy, looks like the clouds decided to move back in. I really don't want a shower before I am ready."

When I came around the corner there was Alice. Well things must have gone faster than I expected. "Hey you. You all done already?"

"Not quite. How is it you can be so freaking cheerful so early? Do you have coffee made? I sure could use something other than that sludge they offer at the office."

"Of course. Come in. You could have just gone on in you know. What is the matter? I can see it all over your face that something is wrong, so spill."

"Johnathon disappeared. We haven't been able to locate him. We did catch several others that were on your list. And we are working on the rest. I am beat! I need coffee."

"Sounds like you need a nap first. Why don't you crash

for an hour or so? I need to look over emails and I promise I won't make a sound."

"That sounds heavenly, but if I lay down now, I won't wake till tomorrow. I only have a couple more hours today and I am headed home. What are you looking at?"

"My friend in Montana sent me an email of her advertisement. I just want to check it and be sure I don't need to add anything."

"Where is it going to be held at?"

"At her store. It is called Water Lilies Metaphysical & Spiritual Shop. It is a really nice little shop. Looks good."

"Have you heard from Annie and Lara yet? Do you think she will be okay?"

"Lara has some exceptional abilities. I will do all I can to help and guide her. Did I mention that I had a visit from her great grandmother and grandmother? They were very happy we found her and the others and just wanted to let me know. But the best part is they themselves had the gift. I truly believe they were the voices I heard encouraging her not to give up. That family has a lot of powerful Mediums. She will have wonderful Spirit guides. Hey! How many scoops of sugar are you going to add to your coffee? Let me dump this and get you another. Are you sure that you should even drive anywhere? Please just lay down for a power nap. I will wake you in exactly and hour."

"Fine. I will lay down. But you have to promise me you will wake me in exactly 1 hour. I need to finish things at the office. You will wake me, right?"

"Yes. I promise. And Jake will stay with you while I go to my office."

"No! You need him to stay with you. I will be sleeping

and there is no reason for him to be with me when you should have him with you. Remember we haven't found Johnathon yet and a few others. So please humor me and just keep him with you."

"Okay. Now go to sleep. You know where the spare bedroom is. I shall come wake you in an hour."

Alice is very worried about those that haven't been found yet. I think I shall seek guidance from Spirit and maybe we will get lucky and locate them sooner. As I was meditating, Spirit showed me something else, that had me very worried. I knew it had something to do with Annie and Lara. I really need to call her immediately.

"Annie? I was wondering if you were planning on going somewhere."

"Charlene. Yes, as a matter of fact we were just talking about going to my aunt's house. A little r & r at the lake. Why?"

"I just don't feel you should go today. Maybe tomorrow. But not today please, I have a bad feeling about this trip. Can you just hold off for a day or so?"

"Of course. I don't see why not. We will just plan it for another day. I really want to thank you again. And Lara would like to say something to you."

"Charlene? I....Thank you so much for helping me. Without your encouragement and help I really don't think I would have made it. I was wondering if after mom and I get back from the lake, would you mind if I came to visit?"

"Lara, I would absolutely love for you to come see me. I have a few things to share with you that I think will help you understand your gift. So yes, please come see me when you feel up to it. I told your mom that you both are welcome anytime. Take care kiddo."

"Thank you so much. And we will. We have so much to discuss. Bye Charlene."

"Bye sweetheart. Be safe and have a blessed day."

As I hung up I felt relief. I am so glad that Annie promised to put the trip off until tomorrow or the next day. Well, I need to clean up and catch up with my day to day business. Put in a call to my mom and family in Alaska. I am sure they have seen the news.

CHAPTER 23

I love driving. Seeing scenery different than what is around my home is so refreshing. Jake is an absolute gem to go on trips with. He takes up the entire back seat and hardly ever needs to stop and go use the trees. This trip is much needed. The news I heard the other night was bad. There just happened to be a horrible wreck on the same highway that Annie would have taken. My heart just stopped when I saw that. Of course I didn't know exactly what Spirit was showing me just that I really needed them to wait a day or so. Very glad she heeded my advice. Now Jake and I are off to Montana and the group meeting there. I have a very good feeling about it.

As I pulled into the hotel, Jake was pretty anxious to exit the vehicle. "Okay boy. Give me a minute to get everything settled. I will return shortly." I looked around and took in the beauty of the surrounding mountains. Montana was a gorgeous state. I walked into the lobby and was pleased with the décor. "Hello. My name is Charlene Ensley and I have a reservation."

"Yes, Ms. Ensley. We have you in a suite, it overlooks the lake and mountains. You also have a balcony. We offer room service or you are welcome to join us for breakfast downstairs. It says you have a pet also?"

"Yes, and he is very well trained. Can you tell me what the deposit will be and my total?"

"Oh. Everything was taken care of already by a Miss Landon. You are all set, here is your room key. Breakfast starts at 6:00 a.m. and we also offer a buffet for dinner starting at 5:30 p.m. each night. Enjoy your day."

"Well thank you. I will." That was an unexpected surprise. I will have to call Julie as soon as I get to my room. "Alright big guy. Let's take you for a walk and then we will go to the room."

As I looked around, a wonderful peace settled over me. I really love Montana. The air is so crisp and fresh. The view is wonderful too. As Jake and I walked I was glad I put the leash on him. It seems there are several squirrels around and Jake's favorite thing to do is give chase. "Not now big guy. We are not at home and I am pretty sure the hotel would frown upon you tearing up the lawn while scampering after the squirrels. Let's just enjoy the walk."

We got settled in and I decided to order a bottle of my favorite wine and then settle into a nice hot bubble bath. Jake was not impressed that I decided to dress his nose with bubbles. But he looked so adorable. Ring…Ring…Ring… "Jake who could be calling me besides Alice? Hello? Oh hey Captain. Is everything okay?"

"Yes Ms. Ensley. I was just calling because I went by your house to check on you and see if you would…"

"You went by my house to check on me? That's sweet. But I am at a meeting in Montana and won't be home for a few days. Was there anything else?"

"No, well, yes. I wanted to ask you out for dinner. But since you were not home I could not do that. When will you be home? And do you have your dog with you?"

"I will be home by October 30th. I love Halloween and I don't want to miss out. And yes, Jake is with me. My bossy friend Alice made sure of it. I realize that there are a few more people to round up so I am being extra careful. But really, I bring Jake all the time. So no need to worry. And Captain? The answer is yes." I said hanging up the phone while laughing. "Oh Jake my boy, I think I am going to like this Captain. I wonder if he knows what I can do. I guess we shall find out if he is okay with it or runs for the hills. Alice seems to like him well enough and you and I both know we will know for ourselves when the time is right. Now, let's play my favorite tunes and to relax."

As I lay back amongst the bubbles, my mind drifted in and out as I listened to my jazz. Would it be so bad to have a man around? He has such kind eyes and he has always been nice to me. I am betting he knows something of what I can do. And if not he will soon enough. It is who I am after all. This isn't high school and all I have to do is walk away if I feel it isn't working out. Just about the time I was ready to drift off, I got a visitor. A visitor of the spiritual kind. Apparently I must have let my mind open a bit too much. Tomorrow's meeting is going to be great. Crud! I forgot to call Julie and tell her thank you. "Well Jake I better get out before my skin decides to stay prune like. Can you bring me my towel please and then scoot on out."

"Ruff," he replied in a quiet bark. Jake knows when we are inside to use a quiet voice.

"Hey Julie. I am all settled in and wanted to thank

you for the suite. You didn't have to do that, but it is much appreciated and Jake thanks you too."

"You are very welcome Charlene. It's the least I can do since you drove all the way here. How is the view?"

As I looked out my window the sun was setting and I could honestly reply, "It is spectacular. Thank you again. So how are we looking for tomorrow night?"

"We have, are you sitting down? 30 people registered! So I am splitting the evenings up into two. I have already emailed everyone with their night. I can't believe we got such a response to the ad. Is this going to be okay?"

"Wow! Of course Julie. You did a marvelous job on the ad by the way. You make me sound more professional than I do. I should have you do all my ads. As long as I have plenty of time to meditate we are good. Did you schedule both for the evenings?"

"Yes. The food and drink is all set, my best friend is catering for me. So no cost there except the buying of said products. Is 15 people going to be too many in one session? We can go 3 nights if you need to."

"No 15 is fine. I can actually do up to 25 in one session. But this will give me more time to be with everyone. I can't thank you enough. Okay I will be saying good night and I shall see you about a half hour before everyone is scheduled to show. Did you let them know to come a few minutes early so they can get drink and snacks and settle in?"

"Yes I did. I am very excited to have you back Charlene. I shall see you tomorrow evening. Sleep well."

As we hung up, I felt a presence behind me. And no, it was not Jake. He was over near the bed already fast asleep and snoring. "Hello. How can I help you?"

Yes I could see him. He was an older gentleman, dressed very stylish for his age. "Hello. My name is Gene. I know that my wife is coming to see you. And I would like for you to let her know that I am waiting in Heaven for her and can't wait to ask her to dance again."

"Okay, I can do that for you. Her name?"

"Marianne. Got to go. Thank you."

And he is gone. Maybe I can get to sleep without any more interruptions. There are many people coming over the next couple days to my meeting. I am expecting many more loved ones to be showing up as well.

CHAPTER 24

The day dawned crisp and sunny. It is getting down to the end of fall and the grass and last of the flowers were covered in sparkles. I better layer clothes for this morning's run. "Well big guy, are you ready to embrace the cool, crisp air? We will just start out on a walk and then put in some miles for our run. But you will have to be on a leash, as we are in the city and it's the law."

"Grrr"

"Yep I know. We will only be here for a couple days. I am pretty sure you can endure for that long. Now let's go."

I was right, it was very cool out this morning but beautiful. I just love taking in all that God has made. Everyone should take time out of their day to just give thanks and enjoy the scenery around them. We passed several people out enjoying their morning walk. Jake and I found a park that had some trails and this is where we decided to run. I let Jake off his leash for this part as we were a ways outside the town. As we returned to the hotel to shower and eat, my phone started to vibrate. Looking at the number, I could see it was Alice. "Good morning. How are you today? Just getting back from our run."

"Morning people make me cranky Charlene. Don't sound so cheerful," grumbled Alice. "When are you getting back? Tomorrow?"

Laughing at my friend, I replied, "No not tomorrow as I have another session. There was so many people signed up we split the meetings. What has you so grumpy today?"

"Mornings. But really, I came to check on your place as I knew you would be out of town. We found some vandalism. They painted your fence with some not so nice pleasantries. But I have already found someone to come and paint it before the weather turns too cold. I just wanted you to know before you got home and were surprised. I think it may be Johnathon or one of the others, but I am not positive. Just please be careful."

"I will and that makes me very angry. We are sure it wasn't kids? It is close to Halloween."

"I am fairly certain. Just promise you will be safe and vigilant."

"I promise. Hey, I wanted to ask about your captain. Is he seeing anyone? He seems like he is a nice enough guy and I don't get any negative feelings off him. Do you like him? I was…"

"Breathe Charlene. Why are you asking me these questions? Is something wrong?"

"Sorry. No there is nothing wrong. I received a phone call from him last night. He called to ask me on a date. And I really like him, even though I don't know him on a personal level. We have only met through you on occasion and mostly during work. So, I suppose I am asking if you would mind that I go out with him."

"Holy crap! He called you? That is surprising. I don't

ever recall him actually dating. He never talks about anyone and he has no pictures on his desk except of his sister and her family and his parents. We have lots to discuss when you get back, so hurry. You have me very curious. Drive safe. Love you much my friend."

"Love you much too. And I promise to be vigilant. So far Jake hasn't been acting up, so I think I am okay here. I will call you when I get close to home."

As I got ready for my first meeting, my mind was wandering and thinking about the captain when I should have been focusing on the gathering. It was silly really. I mean I have dated before. But for some reason my heart was doing double time when I thought about him. Between that and my visitors of the spirit kind, I really needed to double my concentration for meditating.

"Okay Jake, I need you to lay quietly under my chair and just be as Alice says, vigilant. We both know that Johnathon and I am sure many others involved are out there still. So while I am helping others you are going to be my helper."

I arrived to a packed house. The store was set up nicely and smelled heavenly. The food and drink was set out with such a flair as to catch the eye and invite everyone to try a sample. Julie has out done herself. She is one smart business owner for sure. I know she will have many repeating customers from this event and her cousin will for sure gather some new accounts for her catering business.

"Julie, this is absolutely wonderful. You have done a spectacular job setting this all up. I love everything here. I am just going to grab a glass of wine and mingle a bit. When everyone arrives we will get started. Be sure to get names and addresses, like a sign in book and I have put a pile of cards over there by the door, too. And again you have out done yourself."

"Thank you Charlene. I will be sure to put out a sign-in sheet and let everyone know. I can't believe how well this was received. You all good? Do you need anything before we get started?"

"No. Everything is perfect. You go and mingle and I shall do the same."

As I walked around and got a sense of everyone here, I could feel several spirits waiting not so patiently and others that were hanging close to their loved ones. I spotted Marianne off to the side looking like a lost kitten. Her husband was standing watch over her and I could feel his love across the room. Once everyone was here, we all settled in and I introduced myself. Boy many were very nervous that was obvious and we had a few sceptics in the mix. But there were some that looked pretty comfortable too.

"Good evening everyone. My name is Charlene Ensley. Thank you for coming. I hear there was so many people wanting a reading that we had to split the days. I can't thank Julie enough for such a wonderful spread of food and drink. If you have not tried any of the delicious snacks please go ahead and get something. You won't disturb me at all. I also wanted to say thank you for coming. I will get to each one of you in turn. You may ask me questions about yourself, family, or if you want to speak to a loved we can do that too. Well, let us begin."

I looked directly at Marianne and smiled. She seemed very nervous, but when I started talking to her she visibly relaxed. Especially when I described her husband. And let her know what he had to say. To say she was surprised was an understatement. She got teary eyed, but I could see that she was very happy. And Gene himself was content. I think he can move on now that he knows she will be okay. There was another person here that I had passed on the street a couple times while Jake and I were out and about. She was young and a single mother. I could tell she was very timid and scared too. When I concentrated on her, my nose got a whiff of something like sulfur. I told her that I could see a young man next to her and that he smelled strongly of gun powder. She started to cry so hard that it took a good 5 minutes for her to calm down enough to continue. "What is your name?" She was a beautiful young woman and so very afraid of what life has instore for her, that much I could detect. Her feelings were broadcasting loudly. My empathic ability was running high.

"My name is Tara. You can really see him?"

"Yes Tara. He keeps flashing December 12th to me. He says it was the happiest day of his life. Do you know what that date means?"

"That is, I mean was our anniversary. We were married on December 12th. I met Danny just after I graduated from high school. We had been married for four years. We had our baby just over a year ago and six months back, he was in an altercation with the police and he was shot over 27 times and killed!"

She started crying again and Julie brought her a box of tissues. "I am so sorry for your loss Tara. He is telling me that he needs your forgiveness. That he was just trying to provide for you and the baby. He never meant to hurt you. But he also wants you to know that you will be okay. He is saying that he wants you to go to his parents. That they will help you."

"But, he always said his parents didn't want anything to do with him. Why would I bring our baby to someone that didn't want anything to do with him?"

As I listened to what he was trying to convey to Tara, my heart hurt for this young couple who had so much love for each other. "Tara. He is saying that he and his parents didn't always see eye to eye, but that they always loved him. He is very sad that he wasted all this time being angry at them. He needs for you to go to them. They will be sad to hear of his passing but they will welcome you with open arms."

"He is sure? I don't want our baby to be around someone that doesn't want her. I need to know this is absolutely what I am supposed to do."

"I can tell you this is absolutely what he wants. But, he is also needing your forgiveness before he can move on."

"I am so angry at him! But I loved him so very much. Yes. Yes I forgive him. I want what is best for our little girl. I will contact his parents."

"He is now gone. I know that you are scared and undecided about what you will do with your life. But going to his parents, is what is best. I feel you will find your niche there. I see you in a hospital. Helping others."

"Really? I have always wanted to be a nurse. I have already done several classes, but then I got pregnant."

"I truly feel going to his parents will be what is best for you and your daughter. You will be very happy there. And you may not want to hear this now as it has not been very long since you lost your husband. But, I see a man coming into your life. He will be tall and have dark hair. He is in the military and will be in the same line of work as you. Sorry, that is all I see."

"Thank you. I apologize that I have been so blubbery. My emotions are still very mixed up. I will take your and Danny's advice. I feel so much better, like a weight has been lifted. I can't tell you how undecided about all of this I was. You are amazing."

"Thank you, Tara. You will be fine. Okay. Now I am feeling a lady here, she is needing to tell Amber something. Is there an Amber here?"

"Yes, I am Amber. Is it my aunt? My Nana?"

"Well, I am feeling she was very devout in her faith. She is showing me that she spent a good amount of time on her knees praying. And I feel she loves Alaska and the Midwest. Are you from Alaska?"

"Yes, I am originally from Alaska. I have moved here over the last year. But my aunt and grandma weren't catholic. I am trying to understand who it could be."

"Well, I have a feeling that the alarms going off in your house today had to do with her. She knew you were coming and wanted you to ask about them."

Laughing, but nervous, Amber looked at me kind of peculiar. "Well, my fire alarm kept going off. I just purchased it so I know it wasn't the battery. I finally, after the third time of it sounding, pulled the battery and decided it was my aunt, nana or maybe even my husband's grandmother."

"Why would you think that? Have you had readings before?"

"Yes. When I was in Alaska. But only once. I am very curious about the spirit world. I saw this advertisement and decided I would give it a try. I really can't think of anyone that I know that has passed recently. The only person I know that lived in the Midwest and had been to Alaska was my other grandmother. But she passed away when I was 16 years old."

"I see that she has short and kind of curly brown hair with a touch of silver at the sides."

"There is no way that could be my grandma Wilma. Is she kind of round and not very tall?"

"Oh boy she is giving you the look. But yes. She is showing me a hospital. Like she was very sad she had to be there. And that she never got to say goodbye."

"I don't mean to sound disrespectful, honestly. I was so young and we never really got to see my other grandparents as they lived in Washington and we lived in Alaska. But oh my goodness! It has to be her. It has been over 30 years since she passed away. And you are correct that she was in a hospital. She died a very painful death. And my mom barely got there in time before she died. Wow. What could she want? I feel so bad, as the last time I saw her I was pregnant. I really hope she isn't disappointed in me."

"No Amber she isn't. She actually wants you to know that you are a great mom and a fantastic Grandmother. She is very proud of you."

"That is the one thing I wished for my children and grandchildren. That they could have met my other grandparents."

"Oh she has met your children and grandchildren."

"What? She has talked and seen them!"

"No. She has come down from Heaven, she is telling, me to check on them from time to time. She is now ready to go. She just wanted to tell you that she is proud of you and you are a very special mom and grandmother."

"Oh wow. I sure miss her. She has a huge family of grandchildren and great grandchildren and even great, great grandchildren."

"She knows. She is now gone. Anything else you would like to ask me?"

"Well yes. I was wondering if you can tell me if the job I am interviewing for next week is what I should take. Or if I should wait for what I really want."

As I asked Spirit what it was that this lady should do, I got the over whelming feeling of writing. "Well Amber, I think you should go for your dream of writing."

"But how did you know? Never mind, silly question." Laughed Amber.

As I finished up with the other clients, I felt a peace fall over the room.

"Thank you everyone for attending this spiritual meeting. If you will be sure to leave your name and address and pick up a card before you leave. I also do long distant readings. Everyone have a blessed evening."

CHAPTER 25

The meetings went well. Jake and I made great time on the way back to Idaho. We only had to stop a couple times and we had zero problems. When we pulled into my yard Alice's truck was in the driveway. And so was the captain's.

"Hello gorgeous. I am so glad you made it home safe," said Alice while hugging my neck.

"It is good to be home. Montana is getting very cool. Hello captain, how are things at the office?" Something seemed a bit off. Did both of them here mean bad news? "Okay you two. Come in and take a load off. I have been driving for hours and I would love a glass of wine. Are you both staying? I will whip up a simple salad and we can talk about whatever has got you both out here, gracing me with your presence."

"I can't stay. I will just...

"Yes captain, you can. You know it doesn't do any good to say no to me. So sit down and have a glass of wine with us. I promise I won't say anything to put you on edge. Much that is."

Laughing I walked into the kitchen to pour us a much needed glass of wine.

The captain followed me into the kitchen. "You ever been told that you are pushy? I wasn't trying to get out of anything, I just thought to tell you the news and then let you girls have some private time."

"I think you both should stay captain. It would please me immensely. And Jake could use the male companionship, if you don't mind."

"As long as you are sure. How about I take Jake out to play a manly game of fetch while you two girls settle in and fix whatever it is you want for dinner. My name is Greg by the way and I eat just about anything, except..."

"Liver? Yes I know." The look on his face was priceless. "Go. Go play your manly games and I will let you know when dinner is ready." I laughed when he walked out the door. Watching them outside frolicking around through the kitchen window, my heart started a curious little pitter patter. Jake liked him and that was a good sign.

"Earth to Charlene. Come in Charlene. You are a nasty little witch. Give me that glass of wine. Are you sure you want to play that game with him? What if he doesn't like what it is that you do?"

Laughing, I turned and hugged my friend. "I am only teasing him. Just trying to gage his reaction. If I am going to date him, then he will have to know who the real me is. I am not going to lie."

"You wouldn't be lying, much, if you just never told him period. Do you really like him?"

"I do Alice. I really do. You know that isn't the way I am. Honesty in any relationship is key, and I don't hardly ever do relationships because you know how well the past ones turned out. But I have a good feeling about this one. I promise to take it one day at a time. You know I will not jump into something without thinking about it first. Now tell me the real reason you both are here. Is it bad?"

"Actually, it isn't bad news but great news. We have caught the men that were involved in this area. Granted there is so many more in different towns and states. We will be touching base with others and pulling all our resources and information together. We just touched on a very small percentage of this pornography ring. And we have you to thank."

"Yes Charlene. We have you to thank for all your help," said Greg. He came in the back door and we didn't hear him. How much did he hear us talking about?

"Greg." My heart sure does funny things when he is around. "You are more than welcome. I was just helping out a client and then it lead to all of this. I am very glad to have been able to assist in the capture of those bad men. And did you find out how many police officers were involved?"

"We did. At least in this area. Like Alice said, we are coordinating with many other law enforcements around the states. It is a huge operation and I would like to say we will get them all, but only time will tell. As you well know, when we shut down one person another takes his or her place. It is a very sick person that can use women and children for something so perverse."

"I am glad that you are pulling with others to try and stop this. You are correct about there being so many sick people in the world. You can only do so much. Now, would you like a glass of wine or a nice two finger shot of whiskey?"

"I think I will go with the whiskey. Thank you. And your dog, may I say, is very well trained. Did you train him yourself or have someone come in?"

"I did all of Jake's training myself. If Alice hasn't told you yet, we are going to mate her beautiful Lucy to Jake. They will make fabulous partners for your officers or whoever would like to buy one. And they will all be trained out here. I told Alice that my facility is big enough and your men or women are more than welcome to use it for the training."

"No she didn't tell me that. But then again, we don't really talk outside of work. Until now that is. That sounds like it will work out great. Jake seems to be very in tune with you."

I could tell he was fishing for something. "Why don't you just come out and ask me whatever it is you would like to know, Greg." Alice decided at that moment to take said dog out for a walk, so that we could talk.

"I guess, well I know that Alice is your friend and she has never come right out and said what it is that you do or how you know things. But I would like to understand. What is it exactly that you do? How did you know so much about this case?" Alice came in a short time later. We all talked well into the night. Finally, Greg took his leave and Alice decided she had 1 too many glasses of wine and spent the night. I truly think Greg and I will hit it off nicely. He didn't just call me a liar or nut job, so that is a gigantic plus in my favor. My life is going great and I am blessed beyond measure to have such a good friend like Alice. Jake and I both think Greg will be a nice addition to our circle of friends.

CHAPTER 26

The next morning as I was sitting on my back deck watching the morning turn from grey to beautiful pinks and reds, Alice stumbled her way out to the other chair. "Ugh. Why did you let me drink all those glasses of wine?"

"You needed the respite from work and all this mess. You can go back to bed and sleep longer. You don't have to be awake just because I am. I am not going for a run for another couple hours."

"I don't think I have ever had time to just sit and enjoy and actual sunrise. It's kind of nice. I am not rushing to or from a crime scene. And the air smells so nice with your sweet peas all over the place. Sure beats the smell of exhaust. God sure has a way of painting a canvas doesn't He? We heading to church this morning?"

"That would be nice. Are you going to sing me a song? You know I love to hear you sing. It puts my mind at ease. And I am sure that Pastor wouldn't mind at all. I think he would let you sing anytime."

"What does that mean? You don't think he has some kind of crush on me do you?"

She looked a bit panicked at the idea, which made me smile. "He isn't a priest Alice. He is allowed to date you know. Besides, what would be so wrong with dating the Pastor?"

"What would be wrong? I am so not made to be a Pastor's wife. I love church and all but in my line of work, absolutely not. There is no way it could work. Why would you think that?"

Smiling at her I replied, "I never said anything about marriage. I realize your line of work is dangerous and keeps you busy. But there is nothing wrong with just dating. You both have a love for music and truly you both work at protecting and helping others. So you do have more in common that you think."

"What does he do that protects others? I know he loves music, we have sang together before, remember?"

"If you think about it Alice, he does protect people. He shows them the way of salvation and that saves them from an eternity in Hell. Just don't push him away. If or when he does ask you out, I think you should go with it. Give it a try before you decide it isn't for you."

"You know I hate it when you make sense. Can we have coffee yet? You can go get it and bring back some yummy scones so we can watch this spectacular display of color. I need to think now, thank you very much."

"Yes you grump. I will go get the coffee and scones." As I walked into the kitchen, I had the same vision of Alice in a hospital gown. Something was going to happen. That much I knew. I really wished I could see or feel more. Just then she started singing Amazing Grace. I know she did it for herself as much as for me. One of our favorites. I knew that she liked the Pastor, but I didn't realize she was so afraid of having a relationship. I stood quietly to listen and to watch her. She was standing with hands raised in praise and singing her heart out for God. This woman had a voice so rich and pure it gave me goosebumps. "That was so moving. Thank you. I didn't mean to be pushy about the Pastor."

"You weren't. I am sorry that I was a bit grouchy. I don't do mornings well, you know that. And I feel a bit hung over. But I heard you and I will keep my mind and heart open."

"I have a question for you and please don't just say no."

"Shoot," she replied as she took a bite of scone. "Oh these are so tasty. You should open a bakery."

"Have you ever thought about making an album?"

I asked that as she went to swallow and choked on the pastry. Handing her the coffee, she gave me a quizzical look.

"I know that you love what you do and you are very good at it. You wouldn't have to quit your profession, but just record a cd. I know it would sell like hot cakes. Your voice is so soothing. The amount of lives you would help to heal with your music, I am sure would be outstanding."

"You think I am that good? I don't think so."

"I have been blessed with the gift of being psychic and helping others to receive peace and healing. You have been gifted with a voice. A beautiful, rich alto that can touch the hardest of hearts. Every time you sing in church, someone comes forward. You touch them deeply. I am telling you that you should think seriously about it. Pray about it."

"Wow. I never thought about it. I have always sung in church even growing up. But I never gave a thought to putting my voice and music out there for others. First the

Pastor and now my music. Why must you give me so many things to think about?" She said laughing.

"Because I believe in you. And must you forget that I know things others don't? Just think about both. Now I must go run before it is time to leave for church. You going to come with me?"

"Seriously? With my hang over. You are going to kill me girl."

Of course I gave her my best hangdog expression. Works every time.

"Oh sweet baby J. You do that on purpose every time. Fine. I will go with you. But I am going as slow as I want and not a stride faster."

I just smiled and went to change. Life is never boring with my best friend. I have a good feeling that her life and mine are soon to change. I look forward to the challenge.

Printed in the United States
By Bookmasters